Dot'

Colin Payn

ISBN: 9798406943601

Cover design and typography: www.publishingbuddy.co.uk
Editorial: Wendy Ogilvie Editorial Services

1 Fire!

'Mr Banks?'

Rhys took a second as he emerged from a deep sleep, orienting from a very romantic dream into a blackness which he knew, somehow, must be the bedroom. But why was someone phoning him in the middle of the night?

'Yes.'

'Mr Banks, are you the keyholder of Ladywood Park? This is Essex Fire and Rescue Service, and we have a report of a fire on the premises.'

'What? Oh God. Yes, I am the keyholder.'

The noise woke Anne, 'What's the matter, Ree?'

'Mr Banks, we have two appliances on their way, could you meet us there to give access? Would there be any persons on the premises and are there any explosive materials or gas cylinders stored there? We understand, from the informant, that it looks as though it is the building used as changing rooms for football.'

'I'm on my way but it will be another twenty minutes before I get there. There shouldn't be anyone there, and nothing explosive, or gas cylinders stored there. How did it start?'

'We don't know. What about gas services to the building?'

'No, everything runs on electric in the changing rooms.'

Rhys was already out of bed and grabbing for his clothes while talking when the light went on. Dazzled, he saw Anne heading towards her pile of clothes too.

1

'OK, Mr Banks, I won't detain you, please advise us if there is any change of your plans, you will find the number on your phone, but please do not use your phone while driving.'

Rhys cut the call and threw his phone on the bed.

'No, Anne, you are not coming. It's a fire in the changing block. I'll deal with it. You stay here and I'll keep you posted.'

'Like hell. This is a joint project and I'm coming.'

'Not now you're pregnant, it may not be dangerous as we wouldn't be allowed near the fire, but it's dark and you could easily slip or fall over the hoses, or something. I could be there for some time. What is the time?'

'It's four thirty, and I appreciate your concern, but I'm not going to be wrapped in cotton wool for the next eight months or so.'

'Look Anne,' Rhys was struggling to get trousers on over his pyjamas, 'I need you to contact George and the team if we have to close the Park tomorrow, it will be much easier for you to coordinate that from home, plus there are bound to be queries coming in through the website and Facebook. I can't handle all that on my phone. And you could dig out the insurance, plus alert the solicitor. Love you.'

Anne shouted after him, 'Take a torch, and look out for hoses. Love you too. But wait till you get home. I'll give you "pregnant equals redundant".'

By the time Rhys reached the Park he was amazed to see the gates wide open and the blue flashing lights of the fire engines over by the football pitch. Park gardener, Paul, lived not far away and he had been woken by a neighbour, the very man who had alerted the fire service as he arrived home after a nightshift.

'Hi, Boss, it's the roof of the changing area, looks like

it started up there. They are trying to save the walls, but it was well alight by the time I got here.'

'Thanks, Paul. Has it spread towards the tractor shed and office at all, that would be dangerous?'

'No, I told them about that, and they have plans in place to protect it. But I think it's mostly the roof. Luckily it isn't windy tonight so they think they can contain it and put it out fairly quickly.'

Making itself aware above the noise of the firefighters and their equipment was the approaching blues and twos of another emergency vehicle – a police car.

'Hi Paul.' The first man out of the car was a fellow footballer who sometimes played against the Park team. 'And Mr Banks? Seen your picture in the paper a few times, met your Aunt Dot, fine lady. What's happened here? We're here to keep out the public and secure the scene if the Fire Officer thinks it was arson.'

Rhys noticed a few shadowy figures were already gathering by the gates.

'Arson? I hope not, we don't have many problems at the Park, certainly none that would make someone that upset.'

'Well, most aren't, but we'll find out once they've got it under control and then damped down, it looks as though they're winning.'

They had all been watching the flames decreasing as the hoses did their work, picking out any flare-ups immediately until the smoke became thicker and made them cough, as it blew this way and that in the light winds.

Rhys phoned Anne to tell her that it could be some hours before he came home, but the main fire was under control. There was nothing more she could do until about seven in the morning when she could phone round the other members of staff and tell them they could have a lie-in.

Meanwhile, Paul had opened the café and was checking fuses and power before preparing mugs of tea for the firefighters. They said that most of the roof had been destroyed and fallen in but the outer walls, mostly of breezeblock, had survived. Internal stud walls and doors would probably have to be knocked down, but that wasn't a major problem.

What was a major setback was all the toilets for the Park being located at the end of the changing block. Without them the Park would have to stay closed.

2 Consequences

'Once and for all, Ree, being pregnant may mean I've lost control of my bladder, but it doesn't follow that my mental capacity is equally porous. So, don't go making decisions, fluffed out with the latest management speak, about what we need to do, without consulting me. Otherwise, you will witness the biggest hormonal strop the world has ever seen. Got it?'

Anne crashed down her mug, slopping coffee all over the numbered list of actions that Rhys had prepared.

Before he had time to respond Anne had grabbed some paper towel, mopped the bedraggled list, and resumed her complaint.

'We agreed that you suddenly becoming Sales Director of the merged companies meant that I would have to take over running the Park, right?'

Raising his head from the carnage of files, laptop cables and spreadsheets, the dog yawned loudly and looked as though he was considering whether now was a good time to fetch his lead.

Having paused to take a sip of, now cold, coffee, Anne continued her frustrated onslaught, and the dog bowed to the inevitable and went back to sleep.

'I know you're getting used to being the new broom on the block, where everybody hangs on your every word, but it doesn't work here, buddy. I'm not one of your few, and I mean few, women salespeople where you can draw a graph of expected performance drop off as they approach the birth, then flatline for six months while they are on maternity leave.

'My input is up to the hour of birth and starts again as soon as I wake up the next day. About the same time as you start your half of the parental duties, my lad. It's all very well swanning off to America every five minutes —'

'I've only been twice.' Rhys managed to get a word in edgeways.

'In three months, that's near enough every five minutes for me. I hope you got that paternity leave written into your contract; I know it isn't seen as important enough in America for them to make it compulsory. Which is probably why they have so much trouble with gangs and guns, no male caring figure to relate to.'

'That's a bit of a stretch, even for you,' protested Rhys, 'and I did get that done, and I will be there to provide our unnamed little one with words of mature wisdom. And, yes, I admit that I have been applying too much management speak to our situation. So, stop wriggling, go and have a pee, and, on the way back, turn the kettle on. And I'll put all this paper away and we'll concentrate on the little one's inheritance: the Park.'

It was a tribute to their shared history of working in unusual and stressful situations that Anne accepted the suggestion without railing against his diversionary tactic and dictatorial command. Or, maybe it was also the shock that Rhys was thinking as far ahead as their handing over control, of not just the Park itself, but the whole social project, that he'd inherited from his Aunt Dot. With the baby not only unnamed but of unknown sex, as they wanted it to be a surprise, Anne took herself off. She dutifully turned on the kettle on the way back and leaned over the back of the sofa and put her arms round Rhys's neck and lightly kissed him on the ear.

'Right, what's the worst-case scenario with the

changing rooms and toilets out of action?'

Rhys made the coffee and sifted through the pile of papers before replying. 'As far as I can see, for every day the Park is closed it will cost us about fifty pounds more than if we hire porta-loos and open up. Plus, we might be able to claim that back on the insurance. But, even if we open, the football teams won't be able to play so they are not going to be happy. Neither will the tennis players that were able to use the changing rooms when the footballers weren't there. Nor the Chip Notting Twirlers who won't be able to use it to get dressed up for their monthly practice. There will be a lot of unhappy people around for some months unless we can find a temporary solution.

'On the plus side, the fire service has ruled out arson. They are pointing to an electrical fault in the roof, possibly a mouse or rat chewing through a cable, but it was started in a hard to get at part of the roof and they couldn't detect any accelerant, so they don't think it was deliberate.'

Anne had her own laptop open and was looking in dismay at the costs of new facilities. 'Ree, we can't afford these, they run into hundreds of thousands of pounds.'

'I think those decisions are months down the road, knowing how slowly insurance companies work. What we need to decide now is, can we get a temporary replacement changing facility and toilets, or just toilets. Do we hire or buy used? What will the insurance company cover? How soon can we start collecting fees from the clubs again?'

'Yes, I realise that Ree, but looking at these buildings on the internet, we are way behind on providing up to date facilities for the clubs and Park users. We don't have a proper toilet for disabled people, no baby changing places, and when the Twirlers and female tennis players use the changing facilities they have to try to ignore the urinals when they go to the toilets. It's not right. I know Dot won a battle with the Council to build the toilets in the first place, but time has moved on and we'll have to upgrade some way to catch up with the best. I've been thinking about it since we've been to campsites, all the clubs have much better toilets than we do, and I know people have to pay to stay on campsites, but that's not the point. People expect better and our users deserve better. But I'll bet we couldn't afford to upgrade even with the insurance money.'

Unfortunately, during this impassioned analysis of their precarious financial situation, Rhys had dropped off to sleep.

Anne smiled sympathetically, he had been awake, and under strain since four thirty this morning, so she moved all the papers off the settee, lifted his legs on and made him comfortable with a cushion and a quilt. And then reflected that she had been awake all that time as well, dealing with their concerned parents, the Council, numerous Park users and the local paper. Perhaps, on reflection, he had made the right decision to split their resources and each play to their strengths. But she wasn't going to tell him that.

3 New Ideas

Mr Silk, solicitor to the Park, and his wife, also known as his secretary, and aspiring flamenco dancer when on the sangria, sat pondering the insurance policy that he had negotiated.

'Well, it looks watertight; the wiring was all tested when Mr Banks took over from Dot, I have the certificates and sent copies to the insurance company. There have been no alterations or repairs carried out to the building since then, although I suppose wiring can deteriorate with age, but the electrician didn't flag that as something to look out for. Which just leaves what the Fire Officer said, "It could be rats or mice chewing through the wires. That is speculation that we don't want in his official report. Insurance companies can refuse to pay out for damage caused by wild animals, and I doubt one of the staff was secretly keeping a rat as a pet.'

'But does it say that in the policy?' Ethel Silk knew her way round legal documents after so many years in the business.

'Like so many of these things, it does, and it doesn't. Obviously, I made sure they were covered for rodents eating the sacks of seed that are stored in proper metal containers, but it says here, "and other damage". Now, you could read that as "other damage caused while trying to get at the seed", or it could be "any other damage caused by rodents anywhere". Either way I will be phoning the Fire Officer and pointing out that we do not expect anything other than his description of the scene and the possibility that it was caused by an electrical fault. After all, it might have been caused by a spark from a neighbourhood bonfire or a stray rocket.'

'It's July, not November the fifth.' Mrs Silk was clearly not convinced by this line of argument.

'Nevertheless, it is speculation akin to rats in the roof.'

'Or bats in the belfry.'

'Whatever. Obviously I will have to visit the Park and make an inventory of the likely size of the claim and contact their accountant to agree charges for loss of business if the clubs cannot use the Park, and even the café will lose money if the Park has to close altogether. It looks like being a lengthy process to get the figures right.'

'And work out your expenses.' commented his multi-skilled wife, pulling out a handily available brochure for Spanish sun.

At the Park all the staff had turned up to inspect the damage and await the insurance assessor who was due 'soon'.

'The Fire Officer said the structure was safe, although we can't touch anything until the insurance company have poked around. Obviously, the roof has collapsed inwards and that set light to the stud walls, wooden dividers, benches and doors, so there was a massive bonfire but within the walls, so it didn't spread. Which was lucky.' Rhys was one for looking on the bright side.

'My guess is that it will take months to sort out the insurance and the rebuilding …'

'Heat pumps.'

'What?'

'Sorry to interrupt, Boss, but we could fit heat pumps to the new building to save on energy costs and reduce our carbon footprint. And we could install solar panels on the roof, one side faces south, that would save loads on the running costs.' Robin wasn't only a park gardener, he was a passionate advocate of action against climate change.

'Thanks Robin, I have no idea what a heat pump is, but I'm sure you're right that we should look at innovative ideas not just replacing the existing building.'

'We could rebuild so that we had the facilities for a women's football team.' Paul was also beginning to see the possibilities.

'Thank you, Paul. Let's not get carried away, there will be plenty of time to talk about ideas, and their costs, later.

'What I was going to say is that I have spoken to our accountant, Gerry, and we are looking at hiring or buying either toilet, or toilet and changing facilities, as temporary buildings. That would allow us to open the Park, as we need the income from the football teams and the café more than ever. Not forgetting the big contribution from the educational visits, which we need to restart, Robin, can you get on to the schools and explain what is happening?

'Paul, you need to contact the sports clubs, Anne, could you go on the WhatsApp site run by the Park Mothers and keep them in the loop? George, can you get the building fenced off and then work out the best site and liaise with the temporary building suppliers, once we have chosen them?'

Nods all round.

'OK, thanks everybody, I have to go to work so I'll hand over to Anne if you have any queries.'

4 George Earns His Cake

The Park was still looking colourful in the Indian summer of early September, thanks to the flair and hard work of the team led by Head Gardener, George. The kids had returned to school and the background was full of the sound of babies and toddlers still enjoying the warm days. George was happy he was back to his calling of looking after the land rather than his spring and summer role of supervising the competing interests of adults, kids, football and tennis clubs, stray dogs, Health and Safety legislation and Council inspections.

The aftermath of the fire had taken up a sizeable chunk of his time. Once the contractors had been agreed they had needed to clear some land and put in hardstanding before the buildings could be craned into place. All that had taken weeks, and they had to improvise with simple, temporary toilets straight away, just to get the Park open. There were complaints from the sports clubs as the changing area was smaller than the old building, but at least they could get back to their fixture list.

Now he had time to help with the autumn planting alongside the two full-time gardeners, Paul and Robin, and part timer Joss.

Unaware of Anne's condition, something his wife would have spotted straight away, he was happy that the finances and ultimate authority for decisions had passed to Anne, who had taken over running the whole Park now that Rhys was having to concentrate on his full-time job.

As he walked round the lake, noting that the heron was intent on balancing the fish population, once controlled by the anglers, he smiled at the memory of Dot, who inherited the Park, finally banning the fishermen after discovering that his predecessor had been running a side-line in selling fishing licenses not shown on the books, and pocketing the money. Although he missed Dot, her nephew Rhys had certainly managed to put the Park on a better financial footing while maintain the great social atmosphere that he inherited. But Anne had been a revelation. One of the kids who regularly visited the Park had intuitively named her "the future Mrs. Dot". And so it turned out. There was no arguing with decisions Anne made about banning unruly kids or negotiating with the various groups in the Park. Her meetings with the raucous Park Mothers, a notoriously well-informed network who had their own WhatsApp group, supplemented their children's ability to ferret about in places they were not allowed, were every bit as frank as when Dot had met them. Only now they understood the free tea and cakes provided in the café could easily be withdrawn if Anne felt some of them were trying to undermine her decisions...

Having reached the café, George found Anne seated at a table with her disturbing assistant, Mia. It was not that Mia, pretty though she was, flaunted herself in any way, but she had an uncanny effect on men of making them think she was irresistibly attracted to them. She was completely unconscious of this, as Anne had discovered when she interviewed her. Anne had mentioned it to Rhys as a possible reason not to employ her and he had certainly encountered it when he first met her. In fact, he had to warn the gardening team about taking matters in their own hands if male visitors became too interested, as they had all agreed to keep a protective eye on her. Anne had tried to discuss it with her, but it was obvious that Mia had no idea what she was doing or the effect. In all other respects she was an excellent assistant to run the café and she served the female customers with the same friendly smile that drove some of them to ban their partners from going there alone.

Anne looked up when George appeared, a slight frown crossed her face.

'Sorry, Anne, am I interrupting?'

'No, George. It's just that we have a problem with the café – it's doing too well. Let me rephrase that. The café had a poor start with all the bad weather at the beginning of the season, then the rain stopped, and we hit target, but after the kids went back to school, I'd assumed we'd be far less busy, and I could get on with all my other jobs. Then all the mum's rushed back to look at the fire damage and came in the café to sit and discuss what should happen next. And I tell you, we had some weird and wonderful ideas, didn't we Mia? Would you believe someone even suggested building an "escape room" game?

'So now, I'm having to be here almost as many hours, and those other jobs are becoming urgent. I know it will drop off as the days get shorter, but I need, perhaps a month's part time extra assistance, so Mia can call on some help when it gets busy. Any chance you could spare a member of the team to help out?'

George considered that all three members of his team would love to stand around, chatting to Mia and handing out tea and cakes.

'Sorry, Anne. Very busy time of the year for us, all the new bedding plots to be designed and replanted, roses to be pruned, leaves to be cleared and lawn restoration work, kids climbing frames to be inspected and repaired, the lake has to be cleared of weed ...'

'All right, George. You have made your point. I think we will just have to run with restricted opening hours.' Anne patted her stomach, her mind on the 'urgent' job that couldn't be put off as it had an immovable production date.

George thought for a moment, and then put forward the solution that he was unaware had eluded Rhys and Anne all weekend, mainly because of the 'urgent' distraction.

'Anne, when you started the café it was so popular you had your mum and Rhys's mum and dad helping out. They took the required hygiene exams and learned how to serve, use the till, even do some cooking. Have you asked them?'

'George, why didn't Rhys and I think of that?' Anne asked, her palms upwards in disbelief. She turned to Mia, 'let's have tea and cake to celebrate and if any of the lads think George is skiving, we'll tell them it's a crash management meeting, OK?'

5 Going Electric

'Well, good for George, have you sounded out the parents yet?' Rhys was at the other end of a telephone again, God knows where in the country, accompanying his successor sales manager to discuss how the two sales forces had started to work together after the inevitable trauma of losing colleagues as areas were amalgamated.

Anne had phoned round that afternoon. 'They're all very enthusiastic, your mum in particular, you know how she took to it last time, having done some waitressing as a student. And it's only for about a month, so if they take it in turns it will only be a few hours a couple of times a week.'

Rhys sounded relieved, 'You realize that we must tell the staff at the Park about you being pregnant, before one of the parents drops the bombshell. I'm amazed that Joss has managed to keep it secret from them.'

'Of course, I realized that from the moment George mentioned it, and Dad has been as good as gold over separating our private life from working at the Park.'

Joss had been working at the Park part time when Rhys and Anne held their wedding Reception there, and thirty years of Anne having no father changed in a second when Joss went to the aid of her mother, and accidently revealed he was her long lost husband. So, Joss, recovering alcoholic, dosser, and temporary employee, suddenly became Rhys's father-in-law.

Relationships between Anne's Mum, Diane, and Joss had graduated from war to icy, to civil, to an understanding that they would sometimes have to meet at Park events, and now how to behave as expectant grandparents.

'Of course, this doesn't solve our longer-term problem of how we run the Park with you, at best, part time, and me travelling a lot. Still, after four to five years, Little Tot, will be at school.'

'Ree. Wake up, where is your head? Neither of us want our child to grow up as a singleton as we did. In five years, there'll probably be Tot Two and, who knows Tot Three on the way.'

Anne heard the knockon Rhys's hotel door and sighed. 'I hope that's a man with a spreadsheet and not some new friend you have made, with assets.'

'Sorry, love. Back tomorrow, mid-afternoon hopefully. And the man knocking is not happy as I've just told him to let go one of his friends who has used up most of the training budget but didn't improve his performance. It's the part of the job I hate but at least this way he gets a chance to put on his CV that he resigned.

'Love to the Bump and the dog.'

Anne sat back and became aware that the dog's mournful eyes were fixed on her.

'I know, Jem, it's not the same without Ree here is it? Come here and I'll tickle your ears. I know it doesn't make up for the short walk today, but I am so tired with dealing with the Park problems and the parents. Oh, God! I forgot about asking Dad whether he wants to do some table-waiting. He didn't do it last time, but I bet he'll feel left out if I don't mention it.

'Except, he hasn't taken the hygiene exams, so he couldn't do it anyway.

'Hell! Jem, is this what life is going to be like? Me, you, and a one-sided conversation. I suppose it will prepare me for having the baby until he or she can talk.'

It was hard for Rhys as well, he'd always had spells away since they'd met, that was the job of a national Sales Manager, often on the road, training and encouraging his sales force. But he'd hoped he would be more office based in his new role, able to get home every night and relax with Anne to talk over their day's problems and laugh at the odd things that happened in the Park. Instead, the new company owners could call him over to New York to discuss international marketing strategies, new products, or more possible acquisitions in Europe. At the same time, his mind was on how to decorate the nursery and whether he could make the next anti-natal class.

When he arrived home the next afternoon he changed out of his suit and tie, threw his briefcase into the study, and set off for the Park to tell Anne that he'd made one decision, subject to her approval, of course.

'I think we should keep the motorcaravan. I know it's a bit big for you to drive every day and parking can be a problem with that high roof and the blasted height bars that councils will keep putting up but let me explain my thinking.'

Anne paused in clearing the last table in the café and swept her hair out of her eyes to stare at Rhys. Their holiday in France the previous summer, in the very old van, had been a wonderful experience, but a few things would have made it better. An on-board toilet and shower, a heater, a microwave, and power steering. The last was particularly irksome as it was their only vehicle when Rhys was using his company car, so Anne had to use it every day. They hadn't been back home more than a few weeks when an almost new, shiny, fully equipped motorcaravan became a feature on their drive, and they were busy planning new adventures when the twin shocks of promotion and pregnancy hit them.

'I'm not sure I want to be climbing in and out of that when I'm nine months and nine minutes. And what about the baby?'

'I agree, but I've been thinking about holidays with a baby, and the great mountain of stuff we'll need to take with us, and all the trouble with flights and hotels. And then I thought, how much easier it would be if we could get away at weekends or holidays here and abroad, still with all the gear but none of the hassle, like we did in France, but this time with all mod cons on board. I've looked into it, and we can fit a baby seat in the van as easily as a car.'

'But that still means I'd have to drive it every day, and I'd probably need to go to more places where there are multi-storey car parks that I can't get in.'

'Right, so what we need to do, is take the van off the road until after the baby is born, so that we don't need road tax or full insurance and get you a small car.'

There was a silence, rather than the full-blown enthusiasm that he'd expected. Obviously, there was a major flaw in the plan, what had he missed?

'The dog,' said Anne, who came to the answer to his question at the same time, but via a different route. 'If we SORN the van we can't take it out at weekends or days off, and I'd miss our walks with Jem and the fun of making a cup of tea and a snack in the van. And think of the mess he'd make of your car or mine, when we can easily use the cordless vacuum cleaner in the van afterwards. Let's get another car but keep the van ready to drive. You wouldn't save much anyway, and how are you going to keep the batteries topped up and the oil round the engine. Standing on the drive with the engine running for half an hour isn't very good for the environment.

'Oh, and while you were away, I did have a look on the internet for suitable cars and I've narrowed it down to five.'

'What! You mean you'd already thought of all this? And you let me ramble on thinking I'd discovered the answer to at least one of our problems, single handed? Come here and stop giggling like an overgrown schoolgirl or you'll be in detention for a week.'

Fortunately, the definition of detention was not to be revealed, as Mia came out of the kitchen and beamed her disconcerting smile straight at Rhys, which left him temporarily speechless and Anne in further fits of laughter.

'Hello, Rhys. Did you have a good trip? We've been ever so busy, and I keep telling Anne to slow down, in her condition, but she won't listen. Perhaps you can get her to leave more of the clearing work to me?'

That appeal flowed from her eyes, her smile, from her very heart, and Rhys, couldn't resist.

'Anne love, take more care.'

6 Love In Bloom

The summer had been very busy for everybody, but Park gardener Paul had two outside interests that took up all his spare time, his expanding online business, blogging about plants including ideas for garden design, and Sally, "Bubble and Squeak", his on/off girlfriend. There was history between Anne and Rhys and Sally that he could never quite fathom, but she was fun, the sex was inventive, and she understood football, so they had a lot in common.

'Your day off next week Paul, what about a trip to watch Aston Villa at home, I haven't been to see them for weeks?' Sally liked football, but mainly she was Aston Villa's greatest fan, knowing everything from players' boot sizes to the groundsman's children's names.

'Sorry, I've got a planning job to go and see over in Hampstead. Big place, two 'so-called' gardeners, who sound like they can't tell a tulip from a turnip. Could be a good earner.' Paul knew that would have an effect.

'Why don't you take the train up there and meet up with all your friends, make a night of it, I'm sure someone will have a spare sofa you can kip on?'

Sally considered this suggestion for a moment. 'You trying to get rid of me? Got an appointment with a special Rose or Poppy, have you?

'I think I might go; I haven't had a night out with the old gang for a long time.'

Paul considered how much had changed since he met

Sally nearly a year ago. A lot more responsibility at the Park, a growing online business, a feeling that he should push the Park towards a more environmentally aware place. Was he growing old? The noted party animal had stayed with one girlfriend for a year. Unheard of.

And then there was Mia, the girl who naively radiated attraction to all men, the girl he and the others had said they would protect from anyone getting the wrong idea about that smile. The girl who had all the qualities that fun-loving Sally wouldn't understand. The girl who was ten years younger than him. Twenty years if you counted experience of life.

Sometimes he chatted to her after work, while she was clearing up the café and preparing it for the crowds the next day, although she spent more time with his fellow gardener Robin, as they worked on kids' games and treasure hunts that the Park laid on for the summer. But Robin was the only man who had been totally unaware of Mia's eye contact, probably because he doted on his wife and little daughter, always showing photos, and talking about their fun adventures.

'Hi, Mia.'

'Hello Paul. Are you finished for the day?'

'Yes, what about you, nearly done?'

'Anne had some paperwork and I think Rhys is home early tonight so I've got the key to lock up when everything is ready for tomorrow, although I expect it will be quiet as it's going to rain. What will you do if it rains all day?'

'Depends, if it's not too bad we keep working outside, otherwise we have our annual planning meeting coming up so we could all start to put our individual ideas on scraps of paper for the discussion.'

'What ideas have you got? You're frowning Paul, is there a problem?'

'Not a problem, well I don't think it's a problem, but it might be a bit controversial.'

'Is it a secret, or can you tell me? I probably won't understand if it's technical about planting and fertiliser, but I did do biology at college, and we went on field trips and stuff. That's why I applied for the job here. I know it's only in the café, but it's a lovely place to work, like being in the middle of a garden that I don't have to dig. And on my break I always walk round trying to memorise all the plant names, not the Latin ones though.'

As Paul started to explain that he wanted to get Rhys to refocus the Park using the latest ideas to counter climate change, he became aware that his head had been full of conflicts but suddenly a single, clear direction was flowing through his words. He looked up, realising he'd been concentrating on a pebble at his feet. Mia's eyes had changed. No longer the deep, disturbing reflection of some calm inner self, now there was agitation, a flash of excited interest.

'Wow, Paul. Robin would be over the moon with that idea.'

Not exactly what Paul wanted to hear.

'You can't say anything yet, to anybody. I have to work it all out, after all it isn't my Park and Rhys isn't going to take kindly to great ideas that cost a fortune to run. Has Robin said something similar then?'

'Oh, you know Robin, anything to do with the environment and he and his wife and little girl are on the barricades, theoretically speaking. I won't say anything, but it sounds like a fantastic idea. I've always loved those roadside areas in France that are devoted to wildflowers.'

Zones de fleurs sauvages, interrupted Paul. 'Yes, I love them, but you need to walk around them or cycle to get the full effect, no good driving past in a car with the windows closed and the aircon on.'

The fact that Mia's half day and Paul's day off coincided the following week was not a complete coincidence, as Robin had been willing to swap, being good hearted about Paul's plea that he couldn't fix another appointment with his Hampstead client.

Sally, meanwhile, had decided to act on Paul's idea of making her trip a chance for a good drink up with her pals and a couple of days talking about her favourite team.

The lightly made suggestion to Mia that she might like to see how a neglected space could be transformed by proper planning and choice of plants, starting with the unseen canvas of a big Hampstead garden, was well received. It turned out Mia didn't have too many female friends to spend her spare time with, mostly because, one look from her, and boyfriends became terminally distracted.

Paul picked her up outside the Park to avoid any gossip from the Park Mothers.

They drove in Paul's little sports car, a two-seater with an intimacy only a canvas roof could provide. He was dressed in expensive casual style to impress his potential clients.

Mia had changed after her stint in the café, struggling in the little storeroom, but emerging looking stunning in a simple summer dress with a little jacket over her arm for the evening breeze. Anne had eyed her discreet makeup and wondered, but didn't ask.

Paul kept the conversation light-hearted but not personal, after all, this was a business trip with another colleague, not a date, although the low angled seats might have been designed to encourage light dresses to slide imperceptibly away from the perfect pair of knees beside him.

A light twitch and the dress regained its designed length.

'Doesn't your girlfriend usually come with you on these jobs?'

Paul was not sure whether the twitch and the question were connected but decided to play safe.

'Oh, no. Sally doesn't have any interest in plants, gardens or anything outdoors, except her beloved football team, Aston Villa. That's where she is now, spending a couple of days going to the match and then having a drink up with her fellow fans while they discuss whether the goalkeeper had the right colour gloves on to save that last shot.'

'I thought you liked football; you play for one of the teams in the Park, don't you?'

'I like playing, and following the game generally, but that's different from being obsessed with one team. Do I want to know what weight of roller the groundsman might use if it rains the night before the match? Or the fact that the girlfriend of one player has just had twins?'

'Do you think Anne might have twins? I mean, we know things will have to change in the Park, but twins would be amazing.'

Paul tried to look at her to see if she was joking, then look for somewhere to stop, plus put his head in gear, never mind the car, all at the same time. He bumped up onto a kerb with no yellow lines, dislodging Mia's dress again and throwing her lightly against his shoulder.

'Where did that come from? Why should Anne have twins, and what will change at the Park? Do you know what Rhys and Anne are planning?'

Mia adjusted her dress, pulled away from him, despite the angle the car was perched on the kerb, and looked at him with those big eyes that severed his brain from his reasoning.

'I don't know why Anne should have twins, it just seemed a fantastically beautiful idea, the fun they could have growing up together. I have a brother but there's several years between us, I don't think it would be the same as having someone who you grew with for nine months.

'As for the Park, no one has said anything, but I've been thinking about it. Obviously, Rhys can't take over again and Anne will have her hands full, whatever she believes now. So, who'll be in charge? George? I really like George, but he couldn't handle the paperwork or the computer side. And he'll retire soon so why take on extra problems?

'Which leaves two possibilities, as I see it. Employ an outside manager, possibly on a short-term contract, but that's pricey. Or promote you or Robin and bring in Joss to do more days to make up the loss. Which of you could do that, Paul?'

Those eyes, they didn't mesmerise anymore, they spoke to him in the silence that followed, as clearly as if her voice had continued.

He leaned over to kiss her cheek, but she turned and met his lips with hers, but briefly.

'You have choices, Paul. Now, can we get to this appointment before we lose the deal?'

7 A Rocky Path

Mr Khan didn't stand a chance. After calling on the phone at the gates to the property Paul and Mia were met by a 'greeter' who led them from the driveway to the front door, which opened with a faint hum of an electric motor and brought them into an entrance hall so large Paul could have got his flat inside it. Mr Khan stepped forward to take over from the "greeter", and his soft hand shook Paul's, but his eyes never left Mia's face. Paul let go and introduced his associate and Mr Khan held her hand with the delicacy of a connoisseur touching rare porcelain for the first time.

The garden turned out to be almost half the size of the Park gardens, plus there was a swimming pool and a tennis court. Mr Khan introduced them to the two full-time gardeners, who were above the standard Paul had imagined, but their landscaping ability and knowledge of the range of plants was woeful. Paul was amused to notice that Mia kept him between her and Mr Khan, but it was obvious that she had done a lot more than wander round the Park remembering flower names. At one point she even reminded him of an idea he'd mentioned on his blog about a year previously, before painting a word picture of its beauty to an cntranced Mr Khan.

When Paul said the next step was for him to draw up some plans, Mia stepped in to mention that this part of the service was invoiced up front but could be deducted from the final bill if the work went ahead. Mr Khan's expression conveyed that he would have paid the whole thing in advance had she asked, but Mia was looking to a long-term relationship with his wallet.

They had a brief discussion over a cool drink and met Mrs Khan. Mia turned her full greeting smile on to the only person who could stop her husband's extravagance and neutralised the danger by the time the glass was empty, and they said their goodbyes.

'I think that went well, Paul. I know a great pub near here where we can get a drink and a meal, sorry, no alcohol for you as you're driving. And we can discuss how much to charge Mr Khan, in instalments, over the next year. You have a rare talent for garden design, I hope you realise that and ask an appropriate price.'

Paul drove in silence until they pulled into the Old Bull and Bush. Mia kept looking at him apprehensively as they drove, just issuing directions, and finally sitting quite still as he put the handbrake on.

'Sorry, Paul. That was unforgivable. I just took over today, it was your client, your livelihood, your life, and I just steamrollered in. Please just take me home and I won't say another word.

'Except, in my defence. I've never, ever done anything like that before. I do know what effect I can have, but I've never, ever used it before. And today I used it on you because I really do like you. And I used it on Mr Khan because I wanted him to give you the job. And I used my paltry year of business studies to get you a good deal, when you have a degree in business studies and might have been wanting to play it differently.

'I'm sorry, Paul, for all that, but I have never felt so alive as I was being with you today and being your 'associate'. And kissing you. I'm not sorry for that.'

Paul started listening in anger at all the things she mentioned. He had felt used, he had felt undermined, most of all he felt betrayed by that kiss. But, as he turned to reply, he saw the tears running down her cheeks, and lifted his hand to wipe them away.

'Open your eyes.'

She did and looked into his stare. The roles were reversed, he was taking charge of her innermost thoughts, evaluating what he found there, appreciating the agony in her heart.

His hand on her wet cheek slipped round the back of her head and drew her tenderly towards his face, where he held her gaze for a moment longer before kissing her.

8 Green Shoots

George thought he had kept up to date with park management best practice, so he was surprised when both the gardeners, Paul and Robin, raised concerns about how to plan the next year's displays. They'd all worked together so long that their weekly meetings usually resulted in unanimous agreement on ideas even if details were disputed. Often, Joss sat in even if he wasn't due to be working, as he had an encyclopaedic knowledge of wildlife and how plants affected it.

Robin had a real affinity with different soils and conditions under which certain plants would flourish, his own garden was a riot of experimental flowers and vegetables. It was only natural that he was deeply moved by the evidence of climate change and followed events around the world, even going on a couple of demonstrations with his wife and young daughter.

Paul had been "stolen" from the local Council by Dot as he was a superb plantsman designer, with a large following to his website and blog. It was through these connections that he'd gradually become convinced that traditional parks needed to rethink their place in the world of ecological concerns.

Unlike their weekly meetings, the annual discussion on the following year's plans usually took all morning, starting before the Park opened and with Rhys or Anne covering the outside space in case of problems. With Anne and Mia already in the café, organisation was easier this year.

But there was also the fire to consider, not only had the temporary buildings meant a large planting area had to be concreted over but there was the contentious question of what should replace the original changing rooms.

Robin had expanded on his ideas for cutting their electricity bills, even though heat pumps and solar panels were expensive to install in the first place. Now, he was set on improving the building's insulation so less heat would be needed and more of the excess electricity could be sold to the National Grid. Then there was the wind turbine to supply the changing rooms and possibly the office and the café with power at windy times.

Paul was suggesting that creating a proper changing place for women would mean they could use the new building more profitably, as the Women's Football League would provide a second income every month.

George was concerned that all this extra size building and its surrounding paths was eating into the planting area that he regarded as the primary purpose of the Park.

He decided he could do with Management input to the major change to the Park that Paul and Robin were proposing.

'What I suggest is that you write up the plan that we would normally follow, which is really evolving year on year, and then describe the more radical ideas you have suggested and give them to Anne to discuss with Rhys. I'll look at whether any other parks have tried what you're suggesting and add that to the report. Any thoughts you have, Joss, about the effects on wildlife of both schemes would be handy.'

Thus, George had fulfilled his management duties in encouraging innovative thinking, while avoiding the inevitable consequence of having to make a decision.

However, he did give Anne a brief outline of the

situation when they finished, if only to gauge whether he was dealing with shock, horror, or unconfined joy. Perhaps he should have guessed that telling a pregnant woman that they could make the world a better place for future generations, or not, was realistically only going to have one answer.

George began to look up articles on biodiversity, homes for earthworms, underground heating systems for their glasshouses and courses on ecosystems. His wife appeared concerned that he was spending hours studying on the Internet.

'You've only got a few years before you retire, George. Why on earth are you doing all this when you could let the youngsters plan it all and you begin to wind down?'

'Because this is important for our grandchildren, and we could be pioneers in the park industry. And Dot would have been marching with Robin and his family. No, she would have been leading the march. So, when the Park users come to me complaining that their favourite bench has been moved, or there are no pot plants for sale because we are using the space for butterfly-loving plants, I want to be able to tell them just why all the changes are happening. I can't just stand there and say, 'Ask one of the others. My authority would be in tatters.'

'So, what does Rhys say about it?'

'Ahh. Bit of a can of worms there, no pun intended. You know what Anne is like, got to investigate the whole idea now that it's become more personal. So, now she's going on about these trips that Rhys has to make to Europe and sometimes America. He thought the air miles were good, she's now accusing him of deliberately ruining the planet for their child with his unnecessary carbon footprint. Now she's changed her mind on what car she wants; it has to be electric and so we have to get a charging point put in at the Park for her and any other eco

-conscious users.

'As if that wasn't enough of a problem, I've just had a guess at the costings for doing all the things the lads want to do in the Park. There just isn't that sort of money around so Rhys will say no and Anne, usually the prudent one, will go spare. It's tin hat time over the next couple of weeks until they reach a compromise, I can tell you.'

'Who will win?'

'Anne of course. Did you ever see Dot lose a fight? Apart from that stray dog she tried to sue. Well, Anne's made of the same stuff, but God knows where she'll find the money.'

At a time when expectant parents should be happily planning cots and nurseries, there was strife in the Banks household. Talk of planes had downsized to cars and the relative merits of electric models, which grew larger in seating capacity and storage as the extensive list of 'necessities' to transport a baby grew exponentially after discussions with existing parents of young children.

Inevitably, Anne revisited her idea of having the motorcaravan, declaring that her earlier decision to keep it on the road, or have it at all, might have been taken without her having the full facts on diesel-guzzling vans. Rhys countered with the advantages of holidays when they wouldn't be using aeroplanes, and the fact that Euro 6 engines were cleaner than a lot of older petrol engines.

There was an undercurrent to these arguments that, at first, Rhys put down to his old standby, Anne's hormones. But something told him this was different, and he booked a day off, arranged with George to secretly sort out cover at the café, loaded the van with food and water, and surprised Anne with a day out, walking the dog, having a picnic, relaxing away from phone calls and accounts.

After first accusing him of trying to get round her objections to the van, the walk with the dog and the picnic finally made her admit that there was something making her more easily upset than usual.

'Look Ree, I've got everything I could ever wish for, you, a home, family, enough money, the challenge of running the Park, and now the baby on its way. But my heart keeps going back to that other pregnancy, the frightened mother, the little girl, taken away at birth never to know who she really was. Dot had a baby at nineteen, at a time when it would have been a social disaster for her middle-class parents to contemplate.

'Nineteen, Rhys. What were you and I doing at that age? We had the Pill, easy access to condoms and living together was accepted, and babies weren't called bastards any more. So, so different to what Dot went through.'

Rhys held her as she wept silently.

'Now I'm going to have a baby that will be loved by two parents, not abandoned by an unwilling father and then taken away from a distraught mother. I never knew your aunt, but I've met so many people that did, and I've read her diaries. I know she wouldn't have given up that baby without a fight. And now that baby is a woman of about fifty, somewhere in the world, never knowing her birth mother, or perhaps never knowing she existed.

'I'm sorry Ree, I know you think we have enough on our hands, but I think we should try to find that baby, that fifty-year-old woman. Not to involve her in the Park, which we know Dot made sure is legally yours, but to give her back the birth mother that she never knew.'

Rhys was holding her close again, but his mind was full of 'What if's.

What if she didn't know she was adopted?

What if she'd decided not to find her birth mother?

What if she'd found her and didn't wanted to meet her?

What if she was dead?

What if they couldn't find her?

He didn't mention any of these, although he guessed Anne had thought of them already, and dismissed them in her emotional response to their child.

Anne wiped her eyes and reached for her coffee. 'And I love the van and the way you surprised me with a picnic, so no more arguments about that, although it was very devious, Mr Banks. Is there anything else you are hiding from me? Like out-greening me by proposing to turn the Park into a wind farm?'

Rhys laughed, but there was a hint of trepidation. 'Have you any idea what the lads are going to suggest that will turn us into a beacon of self-sufficiency or tackle climate change? I must say I'm a bit worried. Most things I've read about mean a big capital expenditure up front.'

The subject of Dot's daughter was discreetly dropped for the moment, sometimes they needed time to let raw emotion heal before a more practical discussion could take place.

9 Raw Emotions

The 'THUD!' was a floor-shaking feeling of club hammer on brick, repeated over and over, until the cement gave, and the brick started to move. A direct attack on the weaker material changed the sound to the sharp clash of iron hammer on iron chisel and iron chisel on gritty softness.

Joss recognised the sounds, he had worked on many building sites in his years on the road, cash in hand as they never knew when he might move on or be too drunk to turn up.

Now, he was sitting in Dot's old leather chair, deeply engaged between the exploits of wild journeying Odysseus and the duplicitous Penelope fending off the suitors. The general rattle of boots and banter on the floor above was a pleasant background, reminding him he was part of normal society, with all its faults. No longer a faceless collection of rags to be avoided or worse.

The crash of the first brick landing above him made the decision for him, enough reading, it was about time to stand outside the front door and enjoy the urban bustle of his new home and have a smoke. He shouted up to the builders, joking with them that they were supposed to be renovating the place, not knocking it down. They responded, with the pride of craftsmen, that they were only taking the fireplace apart because some cowboy had tried to repair it with unmatched bricks, and they were going to make it look authentic again.

Joss was always in awe of these men, who most people

thought were "just builders", but had skills, an appreciation of historical accuracy and pride in the job that would have amazed the casual observer.

A quiet smoke it was not to be, not with Samuel, the fake Rastafarian from next door. A man who delighted in the uniform of dreadlocks, goatskin coat and rope sandals, but had made his money as a dealer in the City, "First Porsche at thirty, mate", and sent his sons to public school, which he regretted. "Too bloody snooty, 'till they want a handout".

Joss and Samuel had clashed in the past, when it came out that he was a silent partner in the building firm he had recommended so highly to Anne. Joss had stepped in to protect his daughter from a financial rip off and renegotiated the contract from his hard-won experiences on building sites.

A humbled Samuel soon bounced back, and they had become friends as well as neighbours.

'You know that ciggie is more dangerous than a diesel car, don't you?'

'Says the man who used to cloud the road with ganja.'

'Used to, that's the key. I cleaned up my act years ago. Different times, I was never sure Dot didn't have a toke every so often, she was a wild dancer at some of our street parties.'

Joss looked shocked. 'Not Dot. I don't think she needed any stimulants, not when I knew her, she has some wild ideas even when she was getting on.'

'And how are you getting on, Joss? Got Dot's middle floor all to yourself, and a lovely big garden to play with. Which is looking very smart I must say. You need to think about sharing your good fortune. What about your estranged wife? Has she been here yet?'

Joss mumbled something about it being a very busy time, knowing that his neighbour would find an excuse to turn up if he told him Diane was coming for a meal on Sunday.

It had been a breakthrough moment when he suggested it, after they found they were to be grandparents. Their relationship was still frosty, but a baby was a big deal and had forced them to talk seriously about the extra pressure their animosity was putting on Anne and Rhys. The last time he had "entertained" Diane they had been in the Park office shortly after the wedding, their first meeting for nearly thirty years. His contribution had consisted of a packet of biscuits, which were no longer her favourites.

Since then, he had been living in places with modern cookers and had experimented with producing real meals, if only for himself. Sunday would be the real test, and the plates and cutlery, Dot's best, were already polished and covered from any intrusive dust. He worried about wine, obviously he wouldn't drink, but what did Diane like? Then he remembered she would be driving, probably safest to get some water. Still or sparkling? Flavoured? But what flavour? To be on the safe side he had bought eight different bottles.

Then there were flowers, would it be over the top to give her some? He knew that it was seen as an old-fashioned gesture by the younger generation, but he used to buy her flowers when they were living together. Now, buying flowers when he was surrounded by them at work and in the garden seemed silly. But the wrapping and presentation of shop bought flowers had a certain appeal. Should he start from scratch in trying to win Diane back from her new man, or stand aside and let her make decisions without pressure, after all, he had no right to hope that she would ever have feelings for him again?

On the day, he found a rather handsome vase at the back of a cupboard and created a colourful display from the garden and was delighted by Diane's happy reaction. The meal, a mixture of Anne's suggestions and his ability, went well while they managed small talk at the table.

'Joseph, I have something to confess.'

She was still the only one to call him Joseph. They had settled into the comfortable leather chairs, although neither of them could think of any of the furniture, or the flat, as anything other than Dot's.

Diane sat forward, looking a bit sad.

Joss jumped in first. 'If it's about Alistair, you don't have anything to explain. Nothing. You have been living your own life since I deserted you and making a wonderful job of bringing up our daughter. That proves that you have made all the right decisions, and you are perfectly entitled to marry him, you don't have to explain anything to me.'

'Joseph, I am not going to marry Alistair. We have been good friends, more than good friends, but marriage isn't on the agenda. Yes, he has asked me to marry him, but it isn't going to happen. I have told him, at last. He hasn't taken it well, and I think that has confirmed my decision.'

Joss was looking stunned. He didn't like Alistair, not from the moment at the wedding reception when he appeared to be bothering Diane, but that didn't mean Diane couldn't see that he offered companionship and security, and seemingly, love.

But all that was swept away by Diane's next revelation.

'I never did divorce you, Joseph. You were Anne's Dad; I didn't want her thinking you were wiped from that relationship. At least, not until she was old enough to be in a serious relationship herself.

'We are still married, in legal terms, Joseph. That wasn't why I turned Alistair down, if I had loved him, I would have started divorce proceedings some time ago.'

Diane sat back and took a sip of the expensive ground coffee that Joss had prepared and didn't taste anything while she waited for him to react.

His hands were gripping the coffee mug and he had hunched over as though he was staring into its depths, but his eyes were screwed tightly closed and Diane was startled to see him shaking, so much so that the liquid was beginning to wash over the side of the mug. Quickly putting her own drink on the table, she moved to take the mug from his tight grip while resting her other hand on his heaving shoulder to calm him. Unable to prise the coffee from him she was relieved to see that he had stopped shaking so violently but kept her hand on his as she became aware of tears slowly escaping his squeezed eyes.

After a few moments, he opened his eyes, stopped shaking so violently, and smiled weakly until the salty tears reached his lips, and he freed his hand to put the mug down and wipe his mouth on his sleeve.

Diane went back to her chair feeling a bit wobbly. She hadn't expected anything like this reaction. The next sip of coffee made her feel better, even though it was getting cold.

'I'll go and get some fresh coffee.' She collected his mug and went to the kitchen to give both of them space to regroup.

When she returned, Joss had used his newly ironed handkerchief to wipe away the tears and mop the table, so it now looked like a wet brown rag as he stuffed it in his pocket.

'Sorry. My life on the road turned me into a bit of an emotional disaster. Never know how to take good or bad news.'

'Which was this?'

'Both. Good because you thought first of Anne. Bad because you might have sacrificed a happy marriage in all those years. My fault again. So sorry Diane.'

'For goodness sake, stop saying sorry. It was my decision and life has changed. These days people live together without feeling the need to get married. I have lived with a couple of men in all those years. Don't look so shocked, we all have need of loving and they were really good people, both to me and Anne. But I never wanted to marry either of them, so not being divorced didn't arise.

'I didn't expect Alistair to ask me to marry him, but I couldn't ignore it once he had said it, I told him to wait until after Anne was married. That was what he was pressing me about outside the reception marquee when you decided to be a knight in shining armour to protect me, and both of our worlds, sort of, exploded.'

Her explanation ended in an attempt to lighten the atmosphere, and Joss smiled, sensing she was giving him the opportunity to overcome his shock.

But Diane wasn't finished.

'That wasn't really what I wanted to confess. Because confession would be the wrong word, wouldn't it? I didn't do anything I thought was wrong, except that I hadn't told you till now that we were still married.

'My confession was that I came to the Park to see you last week after you finished work, to talk about Anne and Rhys, but you went to a café to meet up with that strange Cattermole woman, and you looked so close that I assumed you were having an affair. After all, she had not long come back from a week in Brighton with the ice cream man and that had caused Rhys all sorts of embarrassment with her husband, the Chief Planning Officer at the Council.

'But then Anne told me you had rung her up to ask her to come along as a chaperone as you didn't want to be alone with the woman. Pity Anne couldn't make it, otherwise I wouldn't have made such a fool of myself, never mind how.'

From looking at her in amazement, Joss started to giggle, then roar with the uninhibited laughter that stirred deeply suppressed memories in Diane.

'Doreen Cattermole! Delusional Doreen we all call her. When she went off with Dennis the Ice cream man, she called herself Cathy and called Dennis, Heathcliff. Dennis is sixty-four and she must be fifty. Unbelievable!

'But, yes, I was a little worried about her intentions. See, she is great with the kids in the Park, they love her stories and the faces she pulls and waving her arms about. Someone persuaded her to write the stories down and send them to a publisher, but he turned it down as it didn't have illustrations. Then, one day she saw me sketching some birds and flowers and that was when she insisted she would meet me after work to discuss illustrating her book. I have said I would have a go with a couple of stories. But me and Delusional?'

He exploded into laughter again and forgot to ask how Diane had made a fool of herself.

Not that Diane would ever tell him that she had gone home, phoned Alistair and he spent the night with her, much to his surprise.

10 Baby Awakenings

The problem with the Park Eco Plan, (PEPup for short as the team couldn't think of suitable U and P words), was a division between the big ideas of Robin, a confirmed climate change warrior, Paul, "small is beautiful for the local community", and Joss whose interest was in anything that worked for the small mammal population.

Robin wanted a Miyawaki miniature forest, a project that would involve the whole community, especially schools, in digging up an area about the size of a tennis court and planting native trees to create cleaner air for the neighbourhood. Paul had designed a series of natural flower beds around the Park with wild species that would attract bees and butterflies. Joss had an idea for bigger hedges for birds and mammals and set aside a wetlands area next to the lake for migrating birds.

George had surveyed the initial draft and pointed out there were no costings, which Robin and Joss saw as an oversight, but Paul, with a business degree, was well aware of. Naturally, they left it to Paul to work out, using their hastily written calculations as a guide. Equally naturally, Paul calculated not only the direct costs of landscaping or buying trees but also the loss of income from taking out a tennis court or reducing other amenities by leaving an area unusable by the public.

Compared with planting a few beds with wildflowers, which needed no work during the year, he concluded that only his proposals would actually save money.

The following week the atmosphere in the meeting

was fraught. Robin, the mildest man in the Park, was distraught and angry that Paul hadn't taken into account the free labour and donations for trees that the community would provide. And, thinking about it further, the publicity value of being one of the first mini forest sites in the country, which would bring visits from scientists and ecology students from all over the country, perhaps from abroad. The reputation of the Park and of Chip Notting would be assured, in fact the Council could be approached for funds as it would enhance the tourist trade.

'Chip Notting doesn't have a tourist trade. Even the church isn't special and no one from Chip Notting has ever been famous.' George injected a bit of reality into Robin's increasingly wild justifications for his plan.

'Well, it's about time the Council woke up and created a reason for visitors to come, otherwise we will end up as a commuter town with no heart.' Robin was in full missionary mode.

Paul needed to calm things down as he had known from the start that finance would rule the outcome, and he really didn't want to see Robin so upset.

'Look, I think Robin has made some good points about alternative sources of finance so we should put those in the proposal and let the Boss and Anne decide.'

Joss was less passionate about his ideas and said he would compromise on the wetlands area if they could agree to adding hedges where there were just fences on the Park perimeters.

The PEPup document, with George's own view that the Park should be changing to meet modern thinking on open spaces, but not detailing a preference among the three ideas, was printed, and given to Anne by the end of the week.

That weekend, having exhausted baby discussions,

Rhys and Anne looked through the proposals.

'Well, obviously the forest idea is out. By the time it was growing well our little Bump, or Bumps, would be almost in secondary school, and even then, I can't see how it would attract any income, even with the interest of eco visitors. And look at the amount of space we would have to take out of use, I can't see the Park Mothers being keen on that.'

'Ree, you must see the bigger picture, it's not about making money, it's about doing what's right for the planet. There is no doubt that, of the three schemes, this would have the greatest effect on purifying the local air for residents, so the Council should support it.'

'Perhaps, but what happens when we have hordes of people wandering about to dig the place up to prepare the ground, all coming by car, no doubt. It could take years to balance that pollution. Then there is the actual planting, more hordes. And the visitors from all over the country, maybe the world, more pollution, more years to offset for the mini forest.

'Now, this area of wildflowers, easy to set up, no maintenance, looks lovely, smells lovely, virtually no cost.'

'But it does nothing for the Park that we wouldn't do already, Ree. These wildflower places are meant to be for roadsides and places which would otherwise just be overgrown with weeds. We should be making a positive contribution to the world, not just substituting two perfectly good growing areas.' Anne was not going to let money have the upper hand now that she was full of new life herself.

'OK. What if we throw in the new hedges for wildlife, that would be an additional benefit for the planet? Or we could stick to what we do best, providing a healthy area for the residents and kids of Chip Notting.'

Anne kicked his foot.

'Don't be so negative. I know, what about some of that stuff we saw at Machynlleth? You know, we went there, the Centre for Alternative Technology. What about wind and solar power to heat the changing rooms and perhaps give us some money back if we have excess energy to feed into the grid? And they did loads of courses and ideas on composting and climate change. We could access their stuff and set up courses for the schools. I'm sure Robin would get over his forest idea if we did something like that. We could even send him on a course there.'

Rhys was still thinking about their precarious finances.

'Hold on, all that stuff costs money up front and take years to pay back. Unless ... Do you remember when we had that financial problem before, Councillor Broome came up with the idea that there were places we could get grants for all sorts of things? What about if we investigate that, he's always ready for a pint, and he did propose to Aunt Dot once, so we know he's on our side? We can't do without Robin for a while though, and we need to talk about the Park staffing for when you have our little bundle to look after, and don't tell me you can do both, superwoman though you are, our baby comes first so we will need someone to take over while you are away.'

Anne was exchanging possible and practical.

'That's six months off. Who knows what might happen in that time? By the way, in all our busy lives, I forgot to tell you that Brenda had a baby last week.'

'What, Brenda from where you used to work? I thought she was tied up with some waste of space, who's name I can't remember, but she was always moaning about him.'

'Dean, that's his name, and he isn't so bad. And, yes,

he is the father. I think Brenda was feeling the biological clock ticking, she's about five years older than me, the magic four 0 just round the corner. I haven't seen her for months, but she phoned to tell me she was pregnant, despite often saying the last thing she wanted was a smelly, wetting baby, as she had one already. The baby is called Riordon, no idea why, it doesn't seem to be a family name for either family.'

'Well, I don't think we should restrict ourselves to family either, whether it's a boy or girl.' Rhys continued with this train of thought, 'And we should probably avoid our initials too, we don't want confusion on our social network spaces, or even snail mail. Have you arranged to meet this smelly, weeing baby any time soon? It would be a good idea to find out the reality of birth and living with a brand-new infant. I have a feeling the leaflets don't give us the full horror, or joy, of the experience.'

'Way ahead of you, according to your diary you are home Sunday, so I'll invite them for the afternoon and tea. If it's still warm we can sit out in the garden, providing you cut the lawn.'

'Not sure I'll have time, but I can ask Robin to come over with the sit-upon mower on the trailer after work one day, we can pay him directly, and I'm sure his daughter would like to play 'homes' in the motorhome.

Rhys considered the arrangement and found a possible flaw.

'What about the café? Will Mia be alright on her own? Or have you arranged for a parent to cover for you?'

'I meant to tell you about Mia. She's changed, after I saw her getting dressed up to go out on her afternoon off. She hasn't said anything, but she has this constant smile, not her 'beam', and she is more assertive, almost bubbling with ideas for how the café could improve next year.

It has to be a man in the background.'

'Don't be so old fashioned, it could be a woman.'

11 Baby Realities

The unseasonable warm weather gave Anne and Rhys the opportunity to have a complete day off from work and the Park, to soak themselves in the idea of the little family they hoped to become in a few months.

Brenda and Dean had transformed from two individuals intent on partying or enjoying the café culture of their North London home, into a couple of droolingly, sweetly proud first-time parents. They also brought enough equipment to service a small hospital, packed into a buggy that looked as though it had been designed by a team of Formula One engineers, complete with three second wheel changes. From having no car, the hybrid estate shouted, 'Massive Safety Features and Off-Road Capability, in Case You Ever Need to Drive Over Hampstead Heath or up Primrose Hill' (both banned to motor vehicles). Rhys noted that the baby was never actually placed in the buggy, he was carried around by one parent or another until the buggy was carefully repacked to go home.

The talk of babies was heavily interspersed with talk at the baby, in an unintelligible language common to all new parents, but less well translated than Klingon. Alcoholic drinks, supplied by the hosts at a scale expected of pre-baby consumption, remained unopened. With one driving and the other breast feeding, the afternoon was soon awash with soft, no calorie drinks, "Preferably from a glass bottle or other recyclable container. We don't want our little one growing up in a polluted world".

Suddenly, it became essential that Rhys should mention the proposals for "greening" the Park, which he'd earlier dismissed as tautology. The fact that it stopped Brenda from completing a long, and detailed, description of the problems of pregnancy was, he thought, worth the risk of extolling the virtues of a scheme which he might be held account for later, when it didn't materialise.

'Yes, an urban mini forest. It will help clean the air and involve the whole community in creating one of the very few places like it in Europe, a great green tourist attraction, with scientific studies of the effects, naturally.'

Anne remained smiling as her eyes met his and threatened retribution with a glance.

'Of course, we might have to lay on an electric minibus from the station, we don't want them to bring their own polluting vehicles to undo all that we want to achieve. And, I expect we'll have a fully interactive media presence so that people from around the world can enjoy it.'

He was gabbling now, the ideas tumbling out faster than his brain could process them, and he could see Anne's smile slowly turning into a malicious grin.

He took a breath and moved to a diversionary tactic. 'Anyway, enough about our Park plans. Dean, you must show me that amazing buggy, I've never seen anything like it, how does it fold down, as it will have to go in the electric car Anne is getting?'

With the buggy being pushed up and down the garden to illustrate its suspension and traction, Rhys managed to get out of earshot of most of Brenda's vivid descriptions of the actual birth. By the time the wheels had been removed and replaced by Dean then, parking it on bricks, the two F1 mechanics were timed taking a side each, the drama of how baby Riordon entered the world was forgotten.

'We must be getting old, we've had a great time and yet none of us had alcohol all day,' Brenda waved as she got in the car. 'By the time me and Anne have both got past breastfeeding, we'll all be bloody teetotal.'

'Hold on, Dean and I are allowed to drink when we aren't driving.' Rhys teetered on the brink of that precipice before adding. 'Of course, only when it is necessary work-related entertainment.' He could feel the knives being withdrawn from his back.

That evening, Anne gave him the edited version of what they had to look forward to if Brenda's experience was typical. What came home to them was that there was no way Anne, or even Rhys, was going to be giving much attention to the Park for at least a few weeks after the birth, even given their belief that they wouldn't be quite as besotted as Brenda and Dean.

'Plenty of time to worry about the Park after Christmas, more to the point Ree, apart from that drivel about growing a whole forest, about as likely as "Birnam forest come to Dunsinane". What are we going to do about the PEPup report the team have produced?'

'Ah, good to see you learned something other than geography. The Scottish play could be inspired, though. Think about it. They didn't actually move trees, just hid behind bits of branch.'

'What are you suggesting? That each visitor is given a bit of tree and then they all stand together and look like a forest?'

'No, that would be silly, but...'

'It would be silly because all the local dogs would come in and wee up their legs.'

'No, will you stop playing Monty Python, and listen. Now, I haven't thought this through because you've only just given me the idea, but instead of digging up a bit of land the size of a tennis court, why not make it linear, using one of the paths and converting it into a tree lined walk, with an aerial rope walk above the trees?'

'I would say that was a genius idea, but for one slight problem. We are talking about planting the trees as saplings, so your rope walk would be about two feet off the ground.'

'We could raise it every year, primary schools first, then working our way up the secondary schools. Let's just say the idea needs more development, and sleep on it.'

Anne wasn't finished.

'You do know that many people think Lady Macbeth got off on her husband killing the king?'

'Right, that's it. Go out of the door, turn round three times and then you can come back in. Or I might cast you as one of the three witches.'

'Hey, Ree, how do you know so much about the theatre stuff, do I detect a frustrated actor that you haven't told me about?'

'Lights and curtain, me, but if you are going to play Lady M then let's pretend the king is dead. Long live the king.'

12 Invasion!

Mia's scream echoed across the Park.

Anne had gone home; it was George's day off and the café was empty as the November afternoon shed gasps of light rain across the landscape. From the entrance came the familiar clang as the big gates, with the wonderful wrought iron, 'Ladywood Park' woven into the design, closed together and Robin jammed the two security spikes into their metal holders.

Nearer to the café, Paul was putting the last of the tools away and looking forward to taking off his heavy mud caked boots.

Before the scream had ended, he was running, his adrenalin fuelled by fear and love, he was round the side of the building in seconds, realising he had dropped all the tools in case he might need a weapon. He stopped momentarily at the overturned table, then jumped the pile of chairs and gathered Mia in his arms as she stood in the doorway.

'I'm OK. I'm OK. Paul, you can put me down, I'm not frightened. It was just a shock when all the chairs and table crashed down, and I saw the cow there. What's it doing in here?'

Robin had made it from the gates, just in time to see the back end of the cow, and Mia trying to bat Paul off. Struggling with which event had made Mia scream, he resorted to an indefinite shout, 'Oyyyy!'

The effect was startling. Paul let Mia go and the cow turned round and knocked another table full of upturned chairs into Paul's legs, causing him to hop around clutching his calf. Now Mia rushed to his aid, holding him close and guiding him to the one upright chair.

Facing a now upset cow, Robin retreated, before catching sight of another beast slowly munching some appetising plants and depositing free manure. A third animal was ambling from the children's play area, obviously intent on confirming that the grass was greener this side of the railings from his field on the other side.

The two gardeners were friendly with the farmer, as far as having a drink down the pub with their neighbour went. But stockmen they were not, and cows, up close, are huge.

Robin backed off, putting the swinging ice cream sign between his fear and the cow's horns, but the initial shock had worn off for the cow, and she was far more interested in the newly planted flower beds, and now there were five cows happily munching away at two weeks planting effort.

Two mobile phones were in action, Robin phoning the police while Paul phoned the pub. Robin got through first and was busily explaining the emergency when he was cut short by the operator asking if any of the cows were on public roads, railways or anywhere else that could put them in danger. Finding they were securely on private property the Police Control Room deemed it not an emergency, despite Robin's anguished cry of 'Sod the cow's safety, I'm the one that's not bloody safe!'

Paul had more luck and was advising, in rather basic language, that the farmer had better get his arse off the bar stool and collect his cows, before the bill for plants, replanting and collateral human injury rose to four figures. Even with three pints under his belt, the farmer could remember that the dividing metal railings were the property of the Park and therefore, undoubtedly, there would be a counter claim of negligence that had allowed his cows to put themselves in danger by eating non-standard greenery.

'Are you two ...?' Robin was beginning to remember the scene with Paul and Mia when he arrived, and their obvious closeness now.

Paul was first to reply, 'Yes, but that's not the point right now, is it?'

'OK. Just saying. So does Bubble and Squeak know?'

'We've split up, but no, she doesn't know about Mia and me. For crying out loud, Robin, never mind about us, go and stop any more cows coming in for an evening snack. I can't go because of my leg. Take the tractor up there and block wherever they're getting in.

'It would happen when the boss is away, and I can't ask Anne to come back in her condition. I'll call Joss, he's good with animals, he told me he'd worked on a few farms in his travelling past.'

By the time the farmer and Joss had collected the cows from various parts of the Park it was dark and the noise and lights of the tractor heaping earth to keep the fence upright, had drawn attention from the neighbours, who had called the police. A persistent banging on the iron gates had a flustered Robin rushing to investigate, to be met by two police cars and half a dozen seriously heavy looking, black clad officers.

'What the hell is going on, Robin?' It was Mark, their local beat copper. 'We got this message that someone was tearing up the Park, lights, shouting, all sorts. Let us in and we'll sort it out.'

'Cows.'

'What?'

'Cows. They got in from the farm, we've had a right carry on trying to find them in the dark and get them back through the fence.'

There were two reactions among the assembled riot squad, one was to burst out laughing, the other was to moan about wasting police time.

Robin was in no mood to take this. 'I phoned your lot first and they said it was nothing to do with them as it was private land. We could have done with a few more bodies to shoo those big buggers off the new plants.'

'Well, we 'd better come in and make sure everything is OK, just so we can write it up.'

In the event, they all ended up in the café where Mia was organising hot drinks for the farmer and Park lads while they calmed down and agreed not to talk about whose fault it was. The moaners on the police patrol were treated to Mia's beam as she gave them their mugs, and promptly decided it was the funniest call out they'd been on in months.

Paul leg had been bandaged by Mia earlier and had been directing operations from his chair, including phoning Anne to tell her what had happened and assure her that everything was under control. He didn't mention the police.

By just after ten, the incident was finished and Robin took Joss home, while Mia drove Paul back to his flat in his car, the first time she had seen it as they had always met at her place while Sally was moving her stuff out.

Anne eyed Mia driving in with Paul the next morning and smiled to herself, then frowned. She may have been right about Mia having found a boyfriend but, a big but, workplace romances that went wrong were bad news in a small organisation. And Paul had form where bed hopping was concerned. And he was so much older than Mia.

Bloody hell, I'm beginning to sound like my mother, she thought. But then it hit her, she was thinking like an employer for the first time since Rhys had left her in day-to-day charge of the Park.

After inspecting the damaged railings, it appeared a cow had decided to use them to scratch its flank and the old foundations had simply given way. The damage in the gardens was mostly cosmetic, the animals had eaten relatively little, snacking their way round the different tastes. With George and Joss taking up the slack as Paul couldn't do much, they had everything back to normal by early afternoon.

Word soon went round the Park Mothers' network and late afternoon a lorry turned up with a couple of husbands, a cement mixer and some 'left over' sand and cement. By early evening the railings were in fresh settings while the farmer placed an electric fence his side while it all dried off.

'Paul, did you mention to the mothers that we needed that work done?'

'I might have mentioned it to Arnie's Mum, she owes me for not asking you to ban the little horror after an incident with trying to get the little kids to go skinny dipping in the lake.'

Anne suppressed a smile. 'And you and Mia, that's a surprise.'

'It was a surprise to me too. But it wasn't just the way she looks at everybody. There are hidden depths to her, very bright and very mature, we have some great conversations, even arguments on serious matters. I know you and Sally had history, not sure why, but she was fun. This is different.'

'Paul, you don't have to explain anything to me. I'm not even a mother myself yet, far less a Mother Confessor. Just be careful with her, I don't want to see either of you hurt.

'I wanted to talk to you about taking on some of the

bookwork while your leg's healing, it will be a great relief to me if you know how things work on the admin side, while I'll be away adding to our home responsibilities.'

'Yeah, Mia said you'd ask me, that's fine.'

'She did, did she?' Anne considered this anticipation of her actions by Mia slightly unnerving. Perhaps Paul was right. If there were hidden depths to this young lady, then maybe she should be more cautious when talking to her about the future of the Park.

That evening she discussed the matter with Rhys, in an almost formal business meeting, as they had agreed to decide on the various proposals for the PEPup greening of the Park.

'I'll go first.' Anne had spent some time with each member of the gardening team, making them justify their proposals in both financial and ecological outcomes.

'Let's clear the decks of those things that we won't be doing. Robin has agreed that his mini forest idea is impractical in the scope of our Park. It would mean removing a tennis court or half a football pitch, involve considerable clearance work and take many years before the benefits of clean air were realised, especially if we factor in the negative ecology effect of all the clearance. On the other hand, his idea of involving the community, particularly the schools, in a Park project to do our bit in combating climate change is still valid.

'Dad's idea of creating a wetland for migrating birds also falls, because of the amount of space needed for it to be viable. It would need half the Park to be effective in attracting the sort of flock sizes he envisaged dropping in for a rest and a snack.

'Paul's cheap and cheerful wild garden is fine in terms of space and cost and immediacy, but adds nothing to existing flower beds, except maybe aiding the bee population. But, with the planting we have already, which is mostly bee-friendly, it would add very little to our green credentials.'

Rhys looked a bit shocked. 'Well, you've just ruled out everything except the hedges round the site being increased in depth. We can't just turn down everything, that would be very bad for morale.'

'I agree, which is why I've been working on a proposal that includes elements from all their ideas. The key is education. We already have school visits every year and Robin and Mia have been doing a great job organising tours of the existing Park, with quizzes and sketch pads, all paid for by the schools. But we could go further and set aside an area where we show elements of a mini forest, a wetland area, a cross section of a hedge with models of the various wildlife found inside. Run interactive displays from wind, solar and water energy, and provide a teaching area for the schools to run their own projects, rather than taking our staff off their normal jobs. I have briefly looked in to grants and other outside funding and it looks promising, but you need to talk to your drinking mate, Councillor Broome to see if he can point us in the right direction.'

'Right, so we don't so much increase our green credentials, as leverage in awareness in the local community so that the overall effect could be greater than anything we could achieve on our own. I like it. And we charge the schools for using the education space, at reasonable rates, of course, and avoid tying up our staff on Park tours. Brilliant.'

'Well, I didn't quite see it that way, Ree, but now you mention it, yes, it's a win win solution. Perhaps we could send Robin on a course, and he could project manage it. He would absolutely love that. Plus, we get loads of good publicity.

'So, what were your ideas?'

'Nothing to beat that, I was still stuck on a different idea of a children's farm experience, possibly involving the farmer next door. But forget that, yours is so much better.'

13 That Other Baby

Halfway through her pregnancy, Anne had read that she should be feeling better after the morning sickness and heightened emotions of the early months. But instead, she began to think more and more about Dot's baby, the lost fifty something woman who was hopefully still alive, and more to the point, still discoverable.

Rhys was at home each evening more regularly now, having assessed the strengths and weaknesses of his regional sales managers he was able to control most things from his London office.

'Ree, can we get in touch with Mr Silk? He was your aunt's solicitor for so long and I know he said he has told us everything that Dot told him, but then he's kept things from us in the past, on Dot's orders. And, before you say it, I know it was fifty years ago, but there might be some clue we could follow up. She's your cousin and someone our little one would normally grow up knowing. I really do want to find her, Ree.'

'Well, I can try, but he did seem fairly convincing about not knowing anything else.'

'Apart from having that sealed box of birthday cards and the birth certificate that Dot told him didn't have the father's name, but still might have some clues, like where was she when the baby was born, and the baby's name.' Tears came again to Anne and Rhys moved to console her, without offering any new ideas about where to start looking.

Mr Silk's office had changed quite a bit from the first

time they had been there to hear about Rhys's inheritance. The underwhelming street entrance had been given a coat of paint to match the new nail bar on the ground floor. The stairs had been cleaned and marked with safety strips, and a handrail and fresh lighting had been installed to help the weary and infirm. On the narrow landing, where Rhys had once feared he could tumble back down, Mrs Silk, affectionately known as Ethel since the wedding, sat at a new desk with a slide out keyboard and elegant monitor.

'Hello, dears, lovely to see you. Looking blooming Anne, all going well? It seems only five minutes from that lovely wedding, well, until the end. Still, it all worked out for the best. And now you're going to have a baby, Dot would have loved to be around for that. She adored kids. Didn't have the foggiest idea of how to handle them in the real world but loved them all the same.'

Rhys jumped in anticipating the tears welling up in Anne's eyes.

'Your demonstration of the actions in the Birdie Song will always remain one of the highlights of the reception, Ethel.'

'Ahhh. Mr Silk was not best pleased with that. I had one or two drinks and then forgot I was drinking gin and not sangria in a big glass. Still, from what I remember it was a great party – until the end of course, but all's well that ends well. Oh, did I just say that?

'Better get you in there in case he starts the clock while I'm chatting.'

The new bookshelves were overflowing with big folders but at least they were no longer in piles scattered around the floor, or leaning up against the workstation, the pride of Mr Silk's entry into the Twenty First century. Not only had the Park provided him with a more secure income but he'd managed to acquire more commercial clients now that he had, belatedly, embraced email and Google.

'Always a pleasure to see you. And Anne, you look positively radiant.'

It occurred to Rhys that Mr Silk had reinvented himself to mirror his name, at last.

Sadly, for all the good feelings radiating from the solicitor, not least because of his charging clock automatically racking up the minutes in the corner of the screen, there was not much new that he could tell them. They fully understood that he couldn't open the sealed box, even just to look at the birth certificate. In her agitated state, Anne had suggested Rhys took Mia to smile at the unguarded solicitor when requesting the opening of the box, but soon accepted Rhys' horrified refusal.

The only snippet they learned was that Dot had let slip that she was at 'UCL' when she fell pregnant. Mr Silk assumed that meant University College, part of the University of London.

'Well, we have a clue at last.' Anne came away from the meeting with a positive energy that demanded action. She announced that, after the Christmas holidays, she would accompany Rhys to London and visit UCL with a determination to discover about Dorothy Flower, who was a student, fifty-five years ago.

In the meantime, her weekly chat with her Mum had been rather odd. Anne had the impression that she'd been crying, but not in a distressed way. Of course, it was laughed off by Diane. 'You're very emotional yourself, that's what's doing it. All that responsibility at the Park and your hormones.'

'Don't talk to me about hormones, Mother. You're changing the subject. I thought you were meeting Dad at the flat sometime soon, have you got a date yet? I've given him some recipes as he was determined to cook for you.'

'I went yesterday, he did a good job, with your help, on the meal, and the place was spotless. But I didn't realise he was so vulnerable. I sort of expected all those years on the road would have hardened him, emotionally I mean. When I told him I had never divorced him, because of you, he went to pieces. He'd thought I was going to tell him I was marrying Alistair, and he accepted that, but then he just sat there and shook, and cried.'

'Mum, Mum. You're crying now, and so am I. When you're ready, tell me what happened next.'

It took a few moments for both of them to regain control.

'Well, I had to hold his shoulder and try to take the cup of tea away from him as he was shaking and spilling it everywhere. He looked so wretched, Anne, he was always so strong, in his determination, I mean. Earlier, we had even managed to laugh about when you were a child and seeing him like that reminded me of some of the good times. But then, to see him so cowed, so … so lost, I suppose is the best way I can put it. He went from Joseph to Joss in that moment, and it was pitiable, Anne.'

'Anyway, we both recovered, but I couldn't stay after that, although I did say that I'd invite him to my flat at some time. Can you make sure he's alright, love? I don't want him going on the booze again, I know he's tried so hard since the wedding. He needs someone and I'm not that person yet, perhaps I never will be. I'm not even sure I want to be – his desertion still hurts. But I want him to become stronger for his own sake. Does any of that make sense, Anne?'

There was a long pause before Anne replied. In that time, Diane could hear her softly crying, and that started her off again.

'Don't worry, Mum, I don't think he'll go back to

drinking again. He almost started after we came home from the honeymoon, bought some cans, but Paul saw him and told us. Ree went round there and gave him a right bollocking, sorry Mum, a right telling off, and made him hand over the beer. Ree is such an old softie, but in his job, he sometimes has to do disciplinaries, so he said he had to forget Joss was my dad and lay down the law. It worked, I don't think Dad has had a drink since, although he still goes to AA.

'Of course, I'll keep an eye on him, I see him at least once a week at work anyway, plus popping round to see how the flat conversions are going. But don't wait too long to invite him round, I bet he's waiting to see if you meant it.'

Rhys was a bit nonplussed to be greeted by a scowling Anne when he got home.

'Ree, do I have a Post it note on my forehead saying, 'Mother – dump your problems here.'

'Oh, yes. Now, Mother, I've got this sales manager ...'

'Shut up. I'm serious. Last week it was Paul on about his relationship with Mia and today it's advising my mum about my dad. It only needs the bloody dog to stand in front of me with mournful eyes, and I'll have the whole set.'

'It's the Bump, you've become the image of Earth Mother, the wisdom of ages is passed down through the female line and you're looked upon as a modern-day Oracle of Delphi ...'

'You don't half talk a load of crap sometimes. And my inquisitors want a direct answer, not some woolly nonsense that could mean anything, or nothing. And I am not living in a cave for anyone.'

Having recounted her conversation with her mother, Rhys considered the worries about Joss for all of five seconds before dismissing them. 'What would be the point of going on a bender when he has two bits of good news, your mum isn't going to wed Alistair, and she's still married to him. I can see him being very emotional, but in a good way, more likely to be more determined to stay off the booze, I would think.

'Actually, it might fit in with what I wanted to talk to you about – Christmas. It's almost December and we haven't discussed what to do about the Park, or our family arrangements. Let's start with the Park. Last year we threw a big party for the local kids, which took months of organising and we got a discount on hiring the big marquee twice, for the party and the wedding. Have you had any thoughts? I know the day to day running has all been left to you, and then there's the baby. If you haven't any ideas, I've had one, during one of my long drives.'

Anne thought quickly.

'Well, I would like us to do something but obviously not a party, I did think we could do something for the local children's hospice, fund some entertainers or buy a really big television, something like that.'

'Great ideas, I hadn't thought of them, so I'll tell you my idea and then we can choose. One of my salesmen has a big packaging contract for a lighting contractor who sends stuff all over the world. One of their lines is commercial size Christmas tree lighting sets and I wondered if we could hook up with the local Council and sponsor some decent decorations for their tree in the town centre. I noticed last year that their set of old bulbs was looking a bit tatty. The new lights are all LED's and can be programmed to flash, change colour, or even respond to music. And they'd be much cheaper to run than the old bulbs. And I could get a good discount.'

Anne considered the idea and began scribbling on her A4 hard backed notebook that was always to hand, for so long that Rhys went to the kitchen, let the dog out into the garden and made two mugs of coffee. It looked like being a late night. He added some biscuits.

As if he hadn't been away, Anne began. 'How busy are you at work? Could you take a couple of days off?'

'I suppose I could … what did you have in mind?'

'We have about twenty regular suppliers at the Park. What about if we got some of them to chip in for a bit of publicity for the lights and then we could afford to get a big television as well for the hospice. That would all take some quick organising, including talking to your favourite Chief Planning Officer at the Council. Then, could you persuade one of the regional television broadcasters to cover the lighting of the Chip Notting Christmas tree and then the kids in the hospice could watch and feel part of it. Actually, I could talk to some of the local suppliers, so you'd only have to talk to the national companies. You might even sell them a box or two while you're at it.'

It was Rhys's turn to take a thinking break so he went to let Jem back in, who insisted on greeting him like he had been away for six months, running round and round barking and covering the floor with smeary swirls of wet mud. Which ensured he wasn't invited into the carpeted room where Anne was busily looking up big televisions.

'Just as well I sounded out Mr Cattermole at the Council then. He had a word with the relevant Committee Chair, and they would be delighted to get some new lights, especially with the cheaper running costs. But we only have seven days to Switch-On night, that's one hell of a schedule. I could probably get the local salesman to pick up the lights and get them down here, I will swing him some extra expenses and they're not too busy at the moment. The problem is going to be the television company, they probably have a fixed schedule up to Christmas and we have to offer them something so outstanding they'll change their plans. Then there's the hospice, I have no idea who to contact and how they'd react.

'I think I need a week off, starting now to get this done. What's the time? I might be able to clear it with both my CEO and America before we go to bed.'

14 Christmas Crackers

While Rhys assumed that getting the OK from the Council was the end of the matter and he could get on with other problems, Mr Cattermole discovered that the Christmas spirit was not abundant when it involved extra work for various departments. For a start, there was the tricky question of how to accept a gift from an organisation that had a commercial service agreement with the Council to provide tractor rental and other minor gardening services. Could it be seen as an inducement to gain more business? A bung, in most people's understanding? That involved the Legal Department.

Then there was the question of insurance in case the tree burned down, or someone was injured. That was Finance.

Did the workforce have the training and skills to set up such a technological advanced product? That was Works.

Were there any staff around in December, when people had been saving up their flexible working hours for months to have a long Christmas break?

An emergency meeting of Legal, Finance, Works, and Planning, ran on into early evening, thus gaining more working hours credits. Ending with no decision meant the Chief Executive had to be informed, much to his annoyance as he was due to meet all the other Essex Council Leaders for their annual consultation, and Christmas meal.

Realising that Dot's successor was likely to be even more put out if his offer was frittered away by internal Council bickering, and visions of having to defend such a mess to Councillors, or worse still, on national television when the inevitable hit the whirly thing, the Chief Executive made an executive decision. If an agreement wasn't forthcoming within the hour, all staff leave in Legal, Finance, Works and Planning would be cancelled until a satisfactory solution was found and the lights were on the tree. And fully working with music, he added, leaving no wriggle room.

Having already ticked the Council off his list, Rhys organised the lights to be delivered the next day, with full instructions. Which left the hospice and the TV station.

Hospice first and easy to contact, easy to visit and explain his mission. But these big televisions were complex beasts and would need someone to make sure they would work with the Hospices' existing internet arrangements. Did Rhys know of anyone who could help them as their man had already flown off to Australia to visit his son?

Rhys thought of Paul who managed the Park computers, but careful to stick to protocol, he phoned George to ask if he could spare Paul for an hour and explained the problem. Paul examined all the circuit diagrams he could find and declared that he didn't have the knowledge to understand the existing complex system of twenty plus televisions, some of which were internet connected, some connected to cameras and some to alarm systems.

'The trouble is you need to use the right cables and switches to get this lot working together. No good just throwing any old co-ax or ADSL cable into the mix, you need someone who understands how it's been put together, so they don't compromise the entire system.'

Rhys returned home and phoned a few likely installers of complex systems, all of whom were run off their feet with domestic work as it neared Christmas.

Anne found him looking dejectedly at the computer and working his way through the Yellow Pages website for increasing distances around Chip Notting.

'Is everybody having a bloody new television for Christmas? There's no point in ordering one until we can get it installed and by then they might have sold the last TV in the country.'

Anne had had a busy day at the Park and had heard from Paul what the problem was that had stumped Rhys.

'Hello, dear. Have you had a frustrating day? While I was wrestling with the accounts, then negotiating with our accountant, refusing the latest demands of the Park Mothers, banning Arnie for a week for throwing the swing over the frame, again, and answering the phone to almost every panicking department in the Council.

'Shall I make you a cup of coffee, Ree? Oh, I see you have one already. So, I'll just get on with cooking the dinner then?'

'I take it you are being a little sarcastic, madam. Come here and have a big hug, while I can still get my arms round you, and then I'll get you a cup of tea. The potatoes are peeled, in the saucepan and salted, the frozen peas are still in the freezer, and I have no idea what else you had in mind to cook, but I've exhausted my culinary skills.'

'Right, the potatoes are a lovely idea, I've never had potatoes and spaghetti Bolognese before, but, who knows, it could catch on. Is it something you had when you were a bachelor? Or is it a throwback to when Mummy let you help with the cooking, and you just fancied carving great chunks out of the poor vegetable?' Anne had lifted the lid on the saucepan, then she went to the food waste caddy and peered in there. 'Oh, there they are, the other half of the potatoes.'

'Will you stop being so sarcastic. It's been a trying day, the Council was OK—'

'No, it wasn't. I've had them on bleating about questions on insurance, overtime, health and safety, do they need three-phase electric, whatever that is, and implying the Park is responsible for their cancelled holidays, if I didn't give them an answer within the hour.'

Rhys looked horrified. 'So, what did you tell them?'

'I said that if they couldn't sort it, you'd be calling the local newspaper and suggesting their incompetence would lead to pictures of little children crying and their parents blaming it all on the Councillors who are in power, at the moment, and that would, no doubt, be brought up at the elections in May.

'Then I had a phone call from the Chief Executive, apologising for the earlier phone calls and assuring me that they would be delighted to receive our gift of new lights and the Council would take full responsibility for everything else.

'So, not only have I been keeping us financially secure but clearing up your leftovers as well.'

'Wow. What can I say? You are the most inventive and competent wife a man could ever wish for.'

'Competent! I'll give you competent. What you could say is, "Darling, I must take you out to dine tonight as you have slaved enough for two of us". And I fancy fish and chips, before you ask. I've had a hankering for fish and chips all day.'

'Fish and chips it is.' Rhys heaved himself off the sofa.

'Oh, and by the way,' continued Anne,' I may have solved your problem as well.'

Rhys fell back onto the sofa, in stunned silence.

'Are we or are we not buying the biggest and most expensive television available? One that is big enough for me to fit diagonally to measure it?'

'We are, well nearly that big.' Rhys agreed.

'Right, so in between sorting out Arnie and the accountant, I phoned a few of our suppliers and got some donations from them against a promise of publicity for the Christmas tree lights.

'When Paul told me what had happened, I spoke to three suppliers of this monster television and mentioned that placing the order was dependent on the hospice being able to install it with specialist expertise. One dropped out with no installer and the other two made offers on a reduced installation price. I said you'd get back to them.'

'For that, Mrs Banks, you get two gherkins with your fish and chips.'

15 Lovesick

It would seem Christmas had stolen up very quickly to several people, not least Paul. He was in a quandary, should he ask Mia to move in with him?

Although it had only been a month since the Hampstead trip, matters had progressed to the point where she'd already stayed over for two weekends and Paul felt more alive than with any other of his many relationships. But that only lasted while she was with him. All the other waking hours were plagued by a tension he'd never experienced before, the nagging worry that she might be upset at something he'd said or not said, or done or not done, and end it.

He'd always been frank with other girlfriends, it was all a bit of fun, and when it wasn't for either of them then there was no point in continuing. And, to be fair, most of them had felt the same way, especially the married ones.

Now, his whole day was consumed with either anticipation for the next time he would see her, even if that was only as he passed the café during work hours, or anxiously rehearsing what he would say when they next met. They tried to keep their relationship casual at work, even though everybody knew they were an "item". But there was always a thrill when their hands brushed, back-to-back, when others could not see. If possible, an excited little clasp of hands shielded by their bodies, then moving apart, another shared memory.

The thrill that ran through him as he drove her home, the first time reaching for her hand as he drove and holding it gently. But he was like a schoolboy on his first date, what he needed was the reassurance that Mia wasn't just giving up her hand, but that she wanted the contact as much as he did. And so, on their second drive, he had laid his hand, palm up on the central consul, and he felt even more adolescent as she immediately placed her hand on his and entwined her fingers, only parting when he had to change gear. Sometimes, they drove miles out of their way, just chatting but with a second conversation of moving interlocked hands providing both a deeper meaning to their words, and the frisson of sexual promise.

After work they often drove out to small towns and wandered along the High Streets, hand in hand, oblivious of their surroundings, always talking, as if there was so much of their past life or their opinions that had to be rushed out in case something should happen to their happy cloud.

He kept wanting to buy her things, if only her favourite chocolate bar, anything to daily prove he was always thinking of her. They had snatched phone calls during each day, disguised as work matters.

'The baker has only left fifteen rolls, let me know if we have many people coming through the gate, and I'll make more sandwiches.'

'I think the Park Mums are plotting something, keep your ears open if they come in the café.'

One day, Anne said Mia could have the afternoon off as it was so wet, and she could deal with any unlikely teas and coffees on her own. It was also Paul's day off and he was doing some work on his website at home. Mia phoned him and he picked her up in his draughty soft top sports car and they found a quiet pub for a meal. The unexpected trip had interrupted Paul's continuing indecision about whether to ask Mia to move in, and he was agitated throughout the meal. When they ran back to the car laughing through the rain, the canvas top and steamed up plastic windows sealed them into a different world, and Paul reached for both her hands and poured out his feelings for her. He hadn't meant to, but it had been building up ever since he'd first seen her and once he'd started he couldn't stop, a love declaration as raw as it was unrehearsed, and ending with his vision of how she occupied a pedestal in his eyes.

Mia was quick to point out that she didn't either deserve or want to be thought of as being somebody on a pedestal. She'd done things she probably shouldn't have done, nothing really bad, but she wanted to be treated as a woman not a goddess.

She held his hands tightly, but by now Paul was panicking. Had he burned his bridges, and would Mia want to walk away from such an all-consuming relationship? In the madness of his words, tumbling out without coherence or editing by his brain, he couldn't really remember what he'd said, but he knew he'd forgotten the big question, would Mia move in with him? He looked into those eyes, those disconcerting eyes that had always been able to hold him in their beam, and now grew bigger, until he was lost in their dark pools and asking without talking and receiving his answer without a sound.

'It's like having two lovesick spaniels around, they've only been going out together for a month and now they've moved into Paul's flat.'

'Anne!'

'What?'

'How long did it take us to move in together? Oh yes. The next day. Never mind a month. What do you think your mum thought of that? She would have been over the moon to have had a month to decide whether we had a chance, and yet here we are, a house, a dog and soon to make her a grandmother. I know you think of everybody connected to the Park as family, but you must give the kids a bit of space to grow and make mistakes. Do you think it is a mistake? Because, from where I'm standing, Paul's wild oats have been widely distributed for years and perhaps a little maturity wouldn't come amiss. As for Mia, she seems like a girl with her head screwed on, young though she is. And a great improvement on Sally, Bubble and Squeak.'

'Says the man who brought her to a party in anticipation of making her squeak.'

'But found his soul mate instead, why do women always have to dredge up the past?'

'Mainly because men have pasts that deserve frequent scrutiny to make sure they don't repeat their mistakes. Look, I agree they make a good couple and they're both ambitious, Mia particularly, she mentioned the other day that she's doing evening classes in accounting and horticulture. I suppose, what worries me is that their ambition will need bigger challenges than we can offer them here on our shoestring operation.'

'I can understand that Anne, and I've given it a bit of thought, in between negotiating the television installation at the hospice and arranging the advertising for our suppliers at the Christmas tree, and contacting the television stations for coverage.'

'Any luck with that, it really would be a shame if the kids couldn't see it after all the hard work?'

Rhys smiled, having at last found an answer to what he had assumed would be the hardest part of the project.

'Well, the hospice has a lot more local contacts than I have, and one of the television executives is on their Board, and I get the impression that there are strings being pulled as we speak.

'Getting back to the Park, in truth, Mia was always going to be a short-term cover for the café, but Paul is important for our future, so we need to concentrate on him first. I know it's still four months off but we're both agreed that you cannot expect to run the Park on a day-to-day basis when we have a young child. Even if I'm at home for part of the time. Sensibly, George wouldn't want to try taking responsibility for the finances, legal stuff, health and safety, Council paperwork, pay and contracts, let alone website development. And he'll be thinking about retiring in the next five years so why take on extra responsibility which would involve learning new skills that are not his natural inclination. Paul is your natural replacement for the time being when our child is born.'

'I think this conversation has taken place between Mia and Paul already,' agreed Anne, 'from hints he has dropped. I think we could fund a salary increase out of my wages, which should be paid as my maternity leave, but we still need to replace him for his work in the Park gardens. Dad is working one day a week, and more to cover when the lads are on holiday so he could take over, if he would agree, and we could use the rest of my salary to pay him.'

Rhys thought that over for a while, his time off work was giving him the opportunity to consider longer-term plans considering the baby's needs now that they'd talked to Brenda and Dean and understood the implications better.

'I think we should consider putting Paul in as General Manager on a year's contract, if as I suspect, he and Mia are thinking of becoming independent garden consultants, or whatever they are called. That would take the pressure off you of the day-to-day running of the

Park while keeping overall control. It would also allow me to look at developing alternative funding streams so that we could either keep Joss on or, if he preferred to work part time, bring in another full-time gardener. Mia could run the café, perhaps with a part timer, or you might want to help in the summer. What do you think?'

'I think you should shut up about the Park, in fact, shut up about everything. Your baby has just kicked me for the first time. Come and feel it.'

16 Parent Problems

Christmas was settled, Anne and Rhys would be entertaining both mums and dads, the dog, and the Bump.

Unless Diane and Joss were still not happy with being together in company. That could be very awkward. Time for a phone call to get it sorted.

'Mother, have you invited Dad to your place yet? It's only three weeks to Christmas and I need to know if there's a problem.

'Oh, and by the way, how do I bake a cake? I know you showed me when I was a kid, but that was decades ago, and I want to do something special for our first family Christmas.'

'A cake? For Christmas? Well, you should have done that at least a month ago to allow time for marzipan and icing to set. Why didn't you ask sooner? We can try, but you'll have to get all the ingredients straight away, I'll email you a recipe.'

'And?'

'And, what?'

'You know what. Have you invited Dad round yet?'

'It's difficult. Alistair has accepted that I'm not going to marry him, but he said we've had such good times together, and we did, so can we still be friends and go out to places like we used to? Now I don't know whether to see Joseph before or after I see Alistair.'

'Mum, you asked me to keep an eye on Dad and he is OK, in fact he is looking happier than I have seen him since he came back to us, and that's you're doing. I'm not asking you to forgive him, but could you please get it sorted so that I can balance Ree and have two of my own parents to eat Christmas cake for the first time in twenty-seven years?'

There was a stifled sob at the other end of the phone.

'I'm sorry, love. I sound like a teenager trying to make up my mind between two boyfriends, when my first job should be to be a mother looking after her little girl. Role reversal. Don't say another word, I'll phone your dad now and you can be assured we'll be perfect guests. And I'll send you a recipe without alcohol for the cake.'

There had to be something about canvas covered small sports cars, for Diane's geriatric MG, with full flow draught around both the canopy and the footwell, proved as claustrophobically catalytic in resolving her situation with Joseph, as had Paul and Mia in their more modern version. But the solution in this case was practical, not romantic. Because Diane lived in North London, she decided to pick Joseph up from his home and take him back to her flat for a meal. That way she could be sure the food wouldn't be ruined by the time public transport got him there. And there would be no rushing everything in case he missed the last bus.

Joseph had never bothered to apply for a new license since his return, although he could drive the tractor round the Park. He'd become used to the modern refinements of Rhys's company car when Anne had taken him out. The MG was a throwback to the cars he used to drive, when he was somewhat slimmer, and he laughed loudly at the trouble he was having contorting himself into the passenger space.

A shadow fell over the interior as he tried to shut the door.

'You're a crafty devil, Joss. You didn't tell me you had a date with this charming young lady. Aren't you going to introduce me?'

Joss sighed. 'Diane, this is my next-door neighbour and pretend hippy, Samuel. Samuel, this is Diane, my ...'

'Nice to meet you, Samuel, sorry to rush, but I have a meal to prepare.' Diane was not going to let that cat out of the bag. The exhaust backfired halfway down the street as she changed up from screaming first gear and took her foot off the throttle.

'What are you laughing at?'

'Oh, come on, Diane, you've got to admit that was funny. I'm still trying to do up my seatbelt and you take off like the Grand Prix lights just went out. I remember you doing that on the bumper cars once. You were waiting for the klaxon to go when the man jumped on the back to collect the money. I held it up for him – and you took off like a rocket and he had to jump off the back. Do you remember?'

'No, you must have been with somebody else.'

'No, I wasn't, it was Brighton, the weekend after we first got together but you were too embarrassed to try and stay at a hotel with me.'

'But you knew how to get away with it, I should have known then you were a flash git.'

'Oh, so you do remember?'

'Just do your seat belt up before we get stopped.'

Later that evening, after Joseph had insisted on trying to help clear up after the meal and ended up standing around uselessly as he had no idea where anything went, Diane asked him what had happened with the strange Doreen Cattermole.

'Well, I told you she'd written all these children's stories, but what I didn't know was how many. There must be getting on for a hundred and for each one she was expecting about ten pictures. Can you imagine churning out a thousand coloured pictures, how long it would take?

And then she tells me that to make them fit the book there are a whole load of dimensions to be kept to. It just got worse and worse.

'But that wasn't the weirdest bit. In order to describe what each illustration should show, I thought I'd just have to read the story. No, nothing so simple. Each scene must be acted out by her so that I could appreciate the different movements she wanted to illustrate. So, we are sitting outside the café in the Council park, where I used to work, and suddenly, she is up and dancing around, miming pouring out tea or showing off a new dress, putting on a crown or brushing her long, pretend, hair. And everybody has stopped eating, the kids have gone quiet, the staff are just standing there, staring, and I'm sat there like a lemon going bright red, no doubt.'

'Lemons are yellow, Joseph.' But there was a smile in her voice. 'So, what did you do?'

'Well, I had my sketch pad with me, and I'd done a few pictures to show her and find out if I was on the right lines, so I asked her to take a look. And, while she was wittering on about colour of dresses and other details it suddenly occurred to me to ask how many stories went in each book and how many books had been agreed by the publisher.'

'And the answer was?'

'Five stories in each book, and none would be commissioned by the publisher until he saw the illustrations.'

'I do hope, Joseph, that you are going to be asking for a share in the profits if your work is equally important as the stories themselves.'

'That's another thing, she has no idea about how it works. She said that if they priced the book at eight pounds then, if they sold a hundred then she would get eight hundred pounds. Now, I don't know anything about publishing, but there must be book printing costs, transport, marketing, all sorts before the publisher makes a profit and then the writer gets his share out of what's left. She might only get a pound a book, so a hundred sales would be a hundred pounds, if I ask for half that would be fifty pounds each. Hardly a fortune.'

'But it would get your name out there as an illustrator if you wanted that sort of thing. So, how did you leave it?'

'I said I'd do the first five stories, but only five illustrations each, that would make it more manageable. And, before you ask, she didn't have any stories that involved her and me.'

'Joseph, more seriously. You know the kids have asked us to their place for Christmas? Well, what you might not know is that they're worried we may make the atmosphere awkward because they are not sure how we are getting on together. After you got very emotional last time, how do you feel about it?

Diane held up her hand to reassure him as he was obviously worried about the question.

'Before you answer, let me tell you how I feel.

'I'm still very hurt with what happened all those years ago, but I have not just survived. I've had a pretty good life and I think of Anne more as a best friend than a daughter, because of the bond we made after you left. I also think you have tried really hard, even before the wedding changed all our lives, to make a new life and earn the respect of your work colleagues. I know Anne loves you and Rhys trusts you, so perhaps I should too. I think we can go as friends, but not Mum and Dad, yet.'

Difficult though it was, Diane kept her eyes on Joseph's face the whole time and watched emotions he could have once controlled like a poker player, course through his features like an open book. This time he managed to look at her when she finished with just a trace of a tear, hastily wiped away, as the agitation subsided, and he was able to speak in a near normal voice.

'Trust has been the most important thing in my life since meeting Dot, she was the first person in decades to treat me as an equal. She inspired the lads at the Park and they accepted and helped me that winter when I was thinking about just giving up on everything. Then Rhys gave me a chance, without knowing who I was, and now you, knowing the worst of me. Anne brought me the first love since I left home, and trust was implicit in that. So, trust is the gold standard for my hopes, and if you can give me that, even on a trial basis, I couldn't ask for anything more. Will you tell them that we'll be coming to Christmas as friends, and can we have another cup of tea, because I'm parched?'

Which gave them both an excuse to smile through misted eyes.

17 Paris Doghouse

If Rhys and Anne were expecting a quiet family Christmas then it was turning into an exhausting, quiet family Christmas.

Rhys's old boss was now on the main Board of the company and decided to get all his Sales Directors together for a Christmas "jolly" – in Paris. Partners were not invited as it was officially a meeting to discuss next year's sales targets and thus tax deductible. But he had sent big displays of flowers, Belgian chocolates, and various bottles of wine to each partner as compensation for "borrowing" their menfolk. All the Sales Directors were men, of course, but he'd failed to ascertain the nature of their partnerships and a few gifts were returned in rainbow ribboned parcels, and there were empty chairs at his feast.

For Rhys it meant missing the weekend of the town lights "switch on" and the unveiling of the giant television screen in the children's hospice. And leaving all the last-minute panics to Anne. Happily, the Council electricians had liaised with the tree lights manufacturers and even the musical colour displays were synchronised to perfection. The tree neither caught light nor fell down, and the television crew turned up with balloons and masses of poppers to add to their broadcast atmosphere.

A special sign on the tree lit up to welcome the children in the hospice and a second camera crew filmed their delighted shrieks as the tree, and then their sign, towered over them on the screen.

Next to the tree stood a life-size plastic gnome in a

Father Christmas hat. It didn't need any advertising, everybody in Chip Notting knew it was the lucky mascot of Ladywood Park and its junior and senior football teams. A hallowed object to be touched on the head for luck by every loyal fan as they trooped into the Park every Saturday.

Anne and Mr Cattermole stood together at the side of the crowd, each with fingers tightly crossed until it was all over, and, with the cameras turned on them, formally shook hands. The Mayor shook hands with Anne, and then Councillor Broome shook hands with Anne, and put his arm round her waist and declared that Dot would have been proud. Anne's extra height just enabling her to avoid his attempt to beerily kiss her on the cheek.

Rhys fared rather worse, if his ashen face was anything to go, by when Anne picked him up from Stansted Airport the next afternoon. After a cursory sales setting meeting, ('Ball park figures, we'll finesse it in January,'), there had been a bus tour of Paris by night, ending at a restaurant about ten o'clock where the multitude of courses and different wines finally ended, and the well rewarded staff decanted the well lubricated sales managers into the coach at about 2 a.m.

It took them to a night club with a cabaret that left little to the imagination, and some of the drinks were bigger than the costumes. By about 5 a.m. Rhys and some others boarded the coach for the hotel, while a few, hardier souls were intent on visiting a little night spot with even more intimate entertainment.

Rhys groaned. 'I'm getting too old for this, at least with our national Christmas "do" I was able to get away early, knowing that they'd be glad to see me go. No one wants to throw up in front of the boss. But last night, that bloody man ...'

'You mean your boss?'

'That's what I said, that bloody man, he was ready to party all night and through breakfast. I could just manage a couple of croissants and strong coffee.'

'Well, I'm glad you didn't let the titillation of the nightclub put you off phoning me at four thirty this morning and murmuring something about swinging tassels and could I buy some?'

'I never did! Did I?'

'Well, you did phone me at four thirty, which was sweet of you to have remembered you were married, and the rest was indistinct, so I think we'd better assume you were at least alone and leave it at that.

'Oh, and the tree ceremony and television crew and the hospice all went off very well, thank you for asking.'

'Oh, God. I'd forgotten that sorry darling.'

Rhys was in the doghouse, from what he could remember, for two days. This consisted of a list of chores which, rather like the Sorcerer's Apprentice in Disney, marched at him in a never-ending queue. Anne relented, and on the third day he was allowed to sleep in, until eight o'clock.

'We're going shopping. It'll make a nice change for you to get out of the house, won't it, Ree?'

Yes, but shopping? If there was an activity Rhys hated more than, "a good spring clean, for Christmas", it was shopping, especially Christmas shopping. What to buy for everybody? Where to get it? Do we spend equal amounts on both sets of parents when we can buy one big thing for the couple that live together, or two smaller things for the ones who don't?

Luckily, he sensed Anne was feeling rather guilty about the penance she had extracted from him for his Paris "fling". After all, in past years she would have been away with the girls and come back in a similar state. So, the present list was prepared, and what hadn't been delivered by the annoyingly convenient but fiscally irresponsible, Amazon, consisted of visiting five shops, but only once each. Another Christmas record. And that included a stop in a coffee shop for a big sticky bun which Rhys regarded as breakfast when he was out on the road as a salesman. Sadly, for his waistline, he also regarded it as an afternoon snack, teatime treat and a sugar rush on a long drive home at night.

'What about Jem? You can't buy presents for everyone and leave the dog out.' Rhys had scored a point here, something his efficient wife had forgotten. Although what you could buy a dog with so many toys that they filled his bed already, he had no idea.

'A stocking!' Anne was triumphant.

'What?'

'A stocking. You can buy a doggy stocking filled with his favourite treats and hang it up Christmas night.'

'Favourite treats? Are there any treats that aren't his favourite, and I don't know where you were thinking of hanging this stocking but over ten feet above him would be the only safe place?

'If you're talking of stockings, I can think of a couple you could slip into that I would like to wake up to on Christmas Day. Or any day come to that.'

'Down boy. Paris has gone to your head, and the Bump might hear you.'

Tranquillity restored in the Banks household, cards piling up on every horizontal surface, the tree planted in a bucket and decorated with baubles and lights, not dancing to Alexa's tunes as Rhys had wanted, but simply flashing in a traditional way, although somewhat more reliably as they were LED lights.

Christmas Day was an enormous success, probably the last one they would celebrate as just a couple for the next twenty odd years if their hopes for several children were realised. Not that there was much alcohol, with Anne's "condition," Joss's abstinence and Rhys having offered to pick them all up and get them home in his rather plush company car.

Anne drew Rhys aside after lunch and commented how well the two in-law couples got on. Diane and Joseph had obviously done a lot of talking and now appeared relaxed with one another, which had somehow released Joss's obvious love of conversation. Whether talking about Dot to her sister and brother-in-law was also a release for both of them Anne couldn't make out, but the conversation flowed easily, and they included Diane in their praise of how well the "youngsters" had coped with Dot's legacy.

There was cake, there was an excited dog wanting to tear the stocking apart with his teeth quicker than scissors, and there was teasing about the naming of the Bump. Speculation about the next Christmas and which would be found wriggling under the pile of wrapping paper, the child, or the dog.

And there was Anne, with a mum and a dad together in her home for the first time in nearly thirty years. Was it any wonder that Rhys found her tearful in the bedroom when he returned from dropping them all off?

18 Anne Triumphs

'You're doing exactly what your aunt did.' Accountant, Gerry, was harsh.

You are treating the Park like a pet project and using your income to do things you cannot afford to do. What's this, in the document you laughingly call a "Forward Projection Plan", about a bloody forest? You can't afford to get your trees lopped properly now, let alone grow more.'

'Yes, but these won't need lopping ...' Rhys was feeling defensive.

'No, but they will need buying, and as I understand this pathetic attempt to fool me, these are going to have to be quite tall saplings. And, I know, because I work for a market gardener, that the cost goes up more per metre for each metre of tree that you want.'

'What, as in metres per second squared, like acceleration of an object that we did at school, except for price, upside down?'

'Precisely.'

'Hold on', Rhys was coming to terms with upside down acceleration, it was just trees that had him puzzled. 'So, are you saying that if I bought a one metre tree for £5 and then bought a three-metre tree, it would cost more than three times as much?'

Even Anne was giggling by now. 'Ree, what century are you living in? Didn't you read the costings on the Park suggestions? My guess is that if a three-metre tree, a much more sensible size for avoiding vandalism, cost

£250 then a nine-metre tree would cost upwards of £4,500. You've got to grow it for longer, dig it up with special machinery, transport it carefully and plant it securely. Would you agree, Gerry?'

'You have been doing your homework, Anne. Why didn't you inject some sense into this farrago of nonsense before it got to me?'

Anne looked at Rhys's face. 'I rest my case. He wouldn't have believed me without your reaction. Thank you, Gerry.'

In the desperate days following news of Dot's Will leaving the Park to Rhys, Gerry had been the only accountant they knew, through boozy nights down the local pub. Even so, he'd blanched when presented with a Harrods's bag full of bills and previous accounts. Without any great expectation of a financial future for himself or the Park, he was surprised to find the project not only vaguely viable but also an interesting challenge. Their relationship had always been based on a "good news" meet down the pub, and a "bad news" meet in the office, arrangement.

The office was modern, quietly efficient, and soulless. Rhys and Gerry wore suits to befit the situation, while Anne looked winter cosy in a skirt and thick jumper that almost concealed the Bump, and she glowed from inner happiness rather than the office heating.

Gerry took the lead. 'So, Anne, you played both of us like an old fiddle, again. Now, where is the proper proposal?'

Two professional looking folders were placed on the desk, one on top of the other, and Anne rested her arms on them, tantalisingly covering the photograph and wording on the cover.

'Naturally, I've listened very carefully to what my husband, and Owner of Ladywood Park, has had to say about his wishes for the future. That is, when he hasn't been flying off to New York or Paris. I have also been through their individual proposals with each of the Park team and, hopefully, kept some of their dreams but with a strong dose of realism.

'There are three substantial changes, the first is around my not being able to cover day to day management functions from Bump delivery for about three, possibly, six months or longer part time. Your main problem, Gerry, is how to recycle my maternity leave payments back into the company to pay for cover by giving Paul more management responsibility and increasing Dad's hours to cover for him.

The second challenge is to monetise the shift from being a class-beating local park into a regionally recognised ecology project at the same time. You'll see I've included a small amount of borrowing to kick start the "green" projects and for changes to signage and, a first, some advertising expenditure for the announcements later in the year of our new status as an ecologically responsible Park. On the basis that borrowing is only a problem if you can't pay it back, I'm forecasting the "green" credentials will open the possibility of an online subscription supporters' scheme, with offers of a few escorted, paying, mini tours of the Park, a newsletter and, perhaps some novelty/green products which can also be sold through the café.

'The third challenge is the rebuilding of the changing rooms after the fire. Thanks to Mr Silk's intervention the cable eating rat theory was left out of the Fire Officer's report, on the basis that no rat remains were found, and other theories, some more fanciful than others, could not be ruled out. But that still leaves an enormous gap between the insurance pay out for the old building and the modern, and extended facilities we need in the Park.

When I say enormous gap, I mean just over one hundred thousand pounds.'

Even Gerry looked shocked, Rhys looked horrified.

Anne continued, 'I know, sounds impossible to spend that sort of money on a changing room, that was my first impression. However, I'm now convinced that we need to spend it if we are to continue to be a great recreational area for local people, but also a beacon site for energy conservation and biodiversity which will attract not only visitors, but funds.

'I am proposing that we rebuild on the existing site using as much of the walls as possible but extending the footprint to include a separate female dressing room with showers and toilets to match the reconfigured male facilities. Also, we keep the public toilets, for Park users, as part of the overall design so that we can minimise the construction and heating costs. The new part of the design is to have a separate outside entrance to a large first floor space that can be hired out to local organisations, small business meetings and eco visitors. We could also run our school visits here. And we could provide food from the café.'

Rhys sat forward as if he wanted to speak, but Anne forestalled him.

'I know what you are going to say, how are we going to pay for all this? I'm just coming to that. One other capital expense first. The building will be heated and lit by a combination of large roof solar panels, an underground heat pump and a wind turbine. This combination should also provide power for the café and the office most of the time. Sometimes we will need electricity from the grid but at times when we are generating more than we need we will be selling it back to the National Grid. We should be in net profit to the tune of several thousand pounds per year if we take into account our previous running costs.

'So, a saving here, a doubling in income from having women's football in the Park, new income from the hire of new facilities and all the other opportunities we have opened for future developments in environmental attractions. Which still leaves a big hole, a very big hole, in how we finance the development before the savings and opportunities kick in.

'And then I found an amazing array of sports money is on offer for organisations such as ours, both grants and long-term loans. While Ree has been swanning off to all part of the UK and abroad, I have been studying these and we could qualify for many of them to do with football, particularly women's football, and upgrading our sports facilities. There is a list of them in the folder Gerry, for you and Mr Silk to look at. Don't forget to add your charges into the proposals, we don't want to be landed with those.

'All this should take us through to next year by which time I'll either be back in full control, or up the duff again, but still in full control. I have prepared the proposals and financial underpinning in these reports for you both. You will need time to study them, so put them in your backpacks and let's go down the pub, where I can have a demure lemonade and drive, and you two can have a pint, or two. You look like you need it.'

The two men did indeed look like dummies, unable to move while their brains took in the full sweep of the proposals.

Anne grinned and stood up to get them moving, Rhys gave her a "well done" pat on the bum. Gerry put his arm round her bulging waist and kissed her cheek, very unprofessional, but appreciated by all.

Strangely, the thing that affected Rhys most was her acceptance that she would be spending a good deal of her time looking after their child after he had to go back to work. In both their worlds it was quite normal for women to expect, and be expected, to be back at work after a couple of months, looking to grandparents or childminders for backup until a nursery could be found.

As for the proposals, perhaps a noisy pub wasn't the conventional venue for detailed business discussion, but they were used to it, and it had turned into a "good news" meeting so a modicum of celebration was allowed by their standards.

Next day, after Rhys had put his "Sales Director" hat on and was driving to work, he mused about recruiting Anne to the company marketing team. The scale from the Park might be different but the imagination and research needed to galvanise it was the same the world over. A woman on the Board, a strong woman at that. He would love to have the power to shake up the mindset of the rather traditional company, especially the American parent.

But it was all fantasy, as he was never going to expose Anne to the uncaring world he lived in, nor put his "soon to be" family at risk of them both becoming results-driven parents. One was enough. How had he missed all that stuff about the Park, the bigger picture about where it was going, where it needed to change? He'd been given the Park and its wonderful community, and he and Anne had embraced it, nurtured it, improved it, but only Anne had seen that it had to change, rethink, as society evolved, even in Chip Notting. Healthy outdoor fun and games would always be wanted, but the kids, like Arnie, were growing away from them, many becoming isolated by increasingly sophisticated games consoles. Would the next generation even come to the Park? Except under duress, and if they could bring their phones to stare at all day?

Perhaps, what they needed was not just to "green" the Park, but use it to inspire interest in "greening" the planet?

Rhys drove into his parking place and looked at the rows of petrol and diesel cars destined to stand there all day, only to drive ten or twenty miles home again at five o'clock, sit there all night, and repeat tomorrow. Like his.

19 Rhys DIY Challenged

Having a charging point installed for Anne's new electric car at the house was easy, the car manufacturer had a link with a company that did all the paperwork and the fitting, and that was all there was to it.

However, the installation of an electric charger unit in the Park was nowhere near as simple. The negotiations started with the Head of Planning, Mr Cattermole, with whom Anne was on good terms after the Christmas tree triumph. He was surprisingly up to speed on the subject having had to look it up when the Council itself decided to put a charging point in its own car park.

'Ahh, yes, the relevant information is contained in Schedule 2, Part 2, Class D of The Town and Country Planning (General Permitted Development) (England) Order 2015 (as amended).'

Anne winced, this sounded like a long haul even if the Council didn't oppose it.

'The good news,' said a smiling, even jovial, Mr Cattermole, 'is that you don't need planning permission from the Council. The Government, in wishing to encourage the sale of electric cars, has decided that, providing it is within certain parameters, closeness to a public road and below a certain height, this will fall under that miscellany known as Permitted Development. I assume you will be putting it in the Park car park, and have it professionally installed, there are strict regulations for that, then I see no reason why it should not be a great addition to your enterprise's offer.' He seemed a little confused at this point. 'Offer or was it offering?' he said, confusingly. He looked up but his gaze was distracted. 'I think that's right, I was sent on one of those courses last week. "The Council is a service company, and its users are customers." It sounds right, except that "customers" usually have choice and can go elsewhere if they are not satisfied. You couldn't have every household choosing their own waste company, could you? There would be lorries going up and down all the roads every day, and bins of all shapes and sizes, some taking plastic waste, some not. What a nightmare. Or what would happen if we turned down a planning consent, but the Council next door would pass it? Chaos.' Mr Cattermole was feeling an ulcer coming on, if his pained expression was anything to go by.

Anne had tried to follow his convoluted reasoning while still recovering from the shock that here was an activity that didn't actually need input from the Council. Just in case she'd misheard, or Mr Cattermole was confused after his modernisation course, she confirmed she could walk out of his office without the usual thick folder of regulations. 'So, you don't need anything from us, and we don't have any forms to fill in for you, is that right?'

'Correct, Mrs Banks, but feel free to drop in with any little queries you have in the future. Always a pleasure to see you.'

Anne wasn't sure whether he was being sincere or had just remembered another part of his "Local Government Management in the Twenty First Century" course.

'How many charging points do you want? We recommend six to start to allow for the upsurge when electric car sales take off. You watch, we'll be rushed off our feet then, might not be able to fit you in for months.

Have you got three-phase?' The salesman was young, smartly dressed and looking towards his monthly sales target.

Knowing she could be out of her depth when it came to technical discussions, Anne had wisely brought Paul along to see various installers.

'I thought just the one, for my car.'

The salesman was ready for that. 'But if your car is stuck on that all day, what about all your visitors?'

'Fair point, Anne, 'specially if we want to attract the green crowd, they'll probably all turn up in them.'

Whose side was Paul on?

But Anne could see the sense of this argument and made her decision. 'Right, then we'll have three. The locals won't use them if they cost money and I can take my car off if we have three long distance visitors, and they will have to swap around if there are too many. Paul, what about three-phase?'

'Well, we would have to get an electrician to run it down to the car park, but we can dig the trench with the digger on the back of the tractor so that wouldn't cost us anything.'

The three of them spent the next hour working out technicalities and haggling over price, at some point Paul muttered something about bringing Mia, which made Anne's eyebrows lift, and a cog of disquiet clicked forward again.

The car was a lifeline for Anne after having the old and then the new motorhomes as her only transport when Rhys was at work. No more worrying about height bars or avoiding multi-storey car parks. They'd chosen a four-door model with plenty of boot space after the visit of Brenda and Dean and baby and clobber. Anne had stipulated sliding back doors for ease of getting kids in and out in confined spaces, she had witnessed the problems of doors wide open while harassed mothers tried to persuade reluctant infants into child seats.

Rhys looked thoughtful when he drove it for the first time being surprised at the acceleration and quietness. Anne forestalled his thinking. 'No good for your job, wouldn't have the range, it would take two days to get to Scotland after two stops for recharging. And that's in the summer, have you seen how quickly the battery drains with the heating, lights and windscreen wipers on in this weather?'

'True, but a hybrid might handle it, I wonder what the economics work out like for a fleet deal? And if cities outside London are going to put in Low Emission Zones, then our salesmen might need them to do their jobs.' Rhys was thinking budgets.

Anne laughed. 'But don't get too carried away with trying to change the tractor in the Park, I'm not sure Paul could survive without his morning coughing fit when that old diesel engine fires up in a cloud of blue smoke.

'Talking of Paul, I've drawn up a job specification for what I'd expect him to do while I'm not around, I'd like you to have a look at it and then I'd like Mr Silk to check it.'

Rhys looked at her, surprised. 'Why do you need a solicitor to look at it? It's Paul, we all know his strengths and weaknesses, Bubble & Squeak to name but one, but he's trustworthy, surely. If there was a problem, I'm sure you two could work it out.'

'If you'd asked me two months ago, I would've agreed, wholeheartedly. But now Mia is with him, and that may be a complication. May not be, might just be my hormones are making my antennae quiver more, but she's a clever girl and I think she can now control her 'beam' and use it to get ahead, at the moment with Paul. So, the more eyes on this contract the better.'

'She's not as clever as my missus though, come here my gorgeous woman with an asset. Only three months to go and our lives will be changed forever. Crikey, you two are heavy.'

'Well, now I have your full attention, as you can't move with me and Bump sitting on you, what's the state of nursery planning? We have the room decision, Tick; we have the baby alarm chosen, Tick; we have the dimmable and multi-coloured room lights selected, Tick; and? ... Nothing that I can see.'

'I've done extensive research on car seats and read every review, and I'm down to the last two.'

'Fine, have you noticed a trend with your involvement with this baby? And by the way, a car seat is not an essential nursery item. All the things you've shown interest in somehow involve technology. For more mundane things, like paint, wallpaper and carpets, a cot even, you don't seem to be interested. If you were, I'd see colour charts and brochures littering the place. Just two points, babies can come early, and pregnant women have been known to have an energy spurt and might feel like grabbing a paintbrush and knocking off four walls without stopping. But obviously that would be a second coat as handyman hubby would have finished everything already.'

'I was thinking of getting someone in to wallpaper it, something plain so that the baby can "express" itself when it's able to hold a crayon.'

'Ree, are you telling me you don't know how to hang wallpaper?'

'I helped Dad once or twice, but he did the fiddly bits, like corners and trimming where it met the coving. I expect I could learn, but we're both busy and what might take me a week, a professional could do in a day, and we do want it to look perfect, don't we? I suppose you're going to tell me you can do it all, smartass.'

'Of course I can, how do you think Mum and I managed all these years? We didn't have any money to employ someone; you should have seen Mum balanced on a scaffold board between two ladders, painting a stair well. And we did all the small electrical jobs, wiring in new plugs and junction boxes. We weren't too happy with plumbing, but we could change a tap, if we could turn the water off.

'I've laid cement, tiled a kitchen, put up bookshelves, even done some soldering, but not too good at that. How the hell do you think I kept those builders to schedule when they were renovating our house? They thought I was the ditsy wife, until I made a few comments about the quality of their work, and how they could be doing it better. They knew of course, just trying to cut corners, running cables up the wall through conduit instead of cutting in and plastering over. That's why I appreciate the work Robin does, even on something like our fence to stop the dog getting out of the garden, he is a craftsman.'

'Wow, Superwoman, I'll throw that trades people directory out then, what a saving, and no call-out fees. Do you take payment in kind?'

'Oi, you. I said I could do it, not that I intended to. Either you learn or keep bringing in enough money for us to employ someone. We both have to learn the next bit together, because neither of us have had any experience of a baby sibling. We've both read the books about the first few months but having Brenda and Dean over for the day was an eye opener to the reality. It was the amount of time and involvement, every minute the baby was awake, that made me decide not to rush back to the Park full time. It was not only servicing, the feeding one end and the cleaning the other, it was the joy they both had in those little daily changes in his behaviour. I decided I didn't want to miss those with our child, even if you had to, at least we could share them each evening, and I can video some on the phone so you wouldn't feel out of it.'

'You know, I quite like you, Mrs Bob the Builder, just don't bend over in your navvies' trousers or you might get a surprise that Bob wouldn't appreciate.'

20 Other Baby Mystery

'If Dot had a degree, then it must be registered somewhere. Oh, why didn't they have Facebook then? We could have found out almost everything about her life from her posts, and cross referenced her friends, where she lived, what music she listened to, everything.'

Anne was becoming increasingly frustrated with her complete lack of progress in discovering more about Dot's young life.

'I found this place called HEDD that does degree searches for employers, but it only goes back to nineteen ninety-nine. Even then they will only confirm or deny information about which college, degree, and year, which the applicant has given. It looks like I'll have to come up to London with you, Ree.'

'Why don't you phone first, it could save you a lot of hassle if they don't have the information.'

'They must have it somewhere and it's too easy to put you off over the phone, much more difficult with a distraught, pregnant lady in front of you.'

However, that confrontation would have to wait as Rhys was called to the European Sales Forecast meeting that was supposed to have taken place in Paris but had turned into a "jolly". This time it was Amsterdam, and some serious work had to be put in by Rhys beforehand, driving around the country and spending time with each regional sales manager.

On her own, Anne felt the loss of his companionship more than ever before, the few months before her baby was due overshadowed by the strangely personal sense of loss of that other child for Dot. In her frustration at not being able to start on the college route, she cast around for another angle to attack the problem and decided that the people who'd known Dot longest were Samuel and Councillor Broome, who both proposed marriage to her. And George, who was her first and most trusted employee.

Anne had never spoken to George about Dot's baby, but he was a quiet and reserved character and possibly, in those early years when Dot was battling the Council and trying to establish the community that was to become her legacy, possibly, her reliance on George may have spilled over into more personal matters.

Every week, Anne had a short meeting with George to sort out any problems and update the future activities diary. When they'd finished and George was putting his papers back into one of his many folders, and Anne had updated her paperless laptop, she asked him to stay as she had a more personal item she wanted to discuss.

Fear ran through George. Was she going to ask him to take early retirement so that they could promote someone, it would have to be Paul or an outsider, to take on the new "green" Park? Or was Rhys so tied up in his new career that he wanted to sell the Park to someone who was willing to run it until the covenant ran out and they could apply to build on it?

'George, were you aware that Dot had a baby when she was at college?'

Relief streamed through George, but then, did this mean there would be someone else with a claim to the Park?

'Err, is there some sort of problem?'

'Oh, George, you did know! All this time and you

never mentioned it. OK, that's a bit unfair, no doubt you were told in confidence and over the years and there was no reason to think it was important, and in the sense, you just asked, no, there is no problem. We've discussed the matter with Mr Silk, and he drew up the Will giving the Park to Ree in the full knowledge that there was a daughter, somewhere, but Dot didn't want her to have any call on inheriting the Park.

'Since we found out, from one of Dot's diaries, I haven't been able to get that poor child – she will be about mid-fifties by now – out of my mind, probably because I know my child will have such a different future. Ree's mum had never heard a rumour about it in the family. Mr Silk cannot tell us anymore, although he has some things in a sealed box, except that Dot let slip one day that she was at a London college when she had the baby. That route is proving difficult to chase up at the moment so I am desperate to find out anything that might give me a clue as to how to contact her, assuming she is still alive or in this country. Can you tell me anything more?'

George was silent as the inner battle raged between loyalty to Dot, and whether, after all this time she would have been sympathetic to Anne's instincts.

'I don't remember much, because it was in the early days when Dot was constantly engaged in trying to keep the Park afloat financially and pushing the Council to let her build toilet facilities within the Park. That was a battle royal, and I was fairly new and had never imagined the way she would fight the Council. Where I came from if the Council said 'No' then that was it. But Dot had this vision, right from the start, that the users of the Park were her family and she would fight tooth and nail to get them the best. Sometimes, we worked together late into the evening trying to read legal books or think up ways of saving money. So much so that my wife wondered what our relationship was, until she met Dot. Then she understood.

'Dot wrung our suppliers dry on their prices, some she pleaded with, others she threatened with rivals. It was very wearing emotionally, and I think she realised that taking on the establishment and some big companies was way out of my comfort zone. But she kept me on board by reminding me that I had a family and if I had to defend them, she knew I would use every trick in the book.

'One evening, we'd completed the figures for the last month and had shown a slight surplus for the first time, and Dot produced this small bottle of whisky and we celebrated with a drop each in our coffee mugs. Only one drink, and it never happened again. But Dot started talking about her family, and I thought she meant the Park users, but then she mentioned her daughter and I think she'd forgotten that I was there. She didn't say a name and I thought at first that she was dead, perhaps in childbirth. But then she said something about how hard it was to watch her grow up without ever being able to tell her that she was her mother. So, I assumed that the child was born before she married and had been adopted.

'I didn't know she'd been a student, or any other details. Dot suddenly seemed to remember that I was there and said something about the Park being her family now so I should understand that was why it had to succeed. And I was never to speak to anyone about her personal life.

'That's all I know, Anne, she never spoke of it again and I didn't even tell my wife, so nothing I've told you adds anything to what you know I'm afraid.'

Anne was smiling, belying the wetness of her eyes. 'You've told me one very important fact, George. Dot knew where her daughter was and could watch her grow up, although from how far away, or how she managed to do it discreetly is the question.

'Thanks, George. And I saw the worry on your face when I said about having a chat. With all the changes that will inevitably take place, I can tell you that you have a job here as long as you want it, so stop fretting and go home to your family and if I find out anymore, I will let you know.'

Next on the list was Samuel, who Anne fortuitously met when visiting her father. The fact was, Joss and Samuel always met on a Wednesday afternoon at a local coffee shop and then returned to play chess at Joss's flat. Anne approached the subject of Dot's baby hesitantly, knowing that Samuel had once felt sufficiently close to propose. Sadly, Samuel had no idea that Dot had ever given birth, but the idea didn't surprise him either.

'Bit of a wild one was Dot when they first moved in here. Liked to have a house full of people, all sorts, including me, when the dreadlocks put most people off. Her husband was OK, but gradually things quietened down. I think he was going up in the world and concerned about his social standing. But Dot, she had obviously been quite fun in her younger days, before she married.

'Now you mention it, there were times when I saw her sitting in the garden, all by herself, looking serious, or maybe sad.'

Councillor Broome was even less help. He hadn't known Dot until she became the owner of the Park and took on the Council. He knew she was a widow and a feisty opponent. Having recently lost his wife, the prospect of having a partner who would provide all manner of excitement rather than a predictable decline, centred around a pub, filled him with a joy that spilled over into an impromptu marriage proposal one night. Naturally, they were in a pub chatting over tactics to improve the Park without getting tied up in Council red tape. He said Dot had turned him down gracefully and bought him a large whisky.

Rhys returned from his trip to Amsterdam to find a happier wife, over her morning sickness and with a couple of Dot's diaries on the settee. She'd told him of her chat with George in one of their frequent late night phone calls, and now she was scouring every entry in the remaining two diaries after Dot left college. Was there any sign that she'd travelled to somewhere on more than one occasion, a clue to where her daughter had been adopted? Sadly not. The entries had become mere records of appointments and meetings, as though the life had gone out of Dot, and she was just doing the minimum social rounds and studying only as much as needed to keep her in college. Anne read desperation in the bleak diaries and wondered if the sealed box held by Mr Silk contained her real writing to her daughter.

21 The Dinner Party

The banging had stopped, the builders tided up and left. Fresh carpets, curtains and all the other furniture and fittings had been restored to the two newly converted flats, and Joss had the place to himself for a few weeks while possible tenants were interviewed, and their histories checked.

He invited Diane round for lunch and to look over the flats before they were occupied. Since the happy Christmas at their daughter's house, they had met once at a café, as Diane was popping into the Park to visit Anne and thought it would be a good idea to test how she felt about Joseph away from the family group. The café was convenient, but held conflicting memories for Diane, as it was the place she had seen him with Doreen Cattermole, and assumed the worst.

Contrary to her concerns about him taking up drinking again, he had, as Anne predicted, become happier and more focussed in his spare time. He'd abandoned his second-hand laptop and bought himself a desktop which sat proudly on Dot's solid old desk in the flat. His big hands coped so much better with a full-sized keyboard as he pecked away at ideas for the Park, his minimal accounts and his steadily increasing collection of photographs of wildlife. The revelation of digital cameras, not needing to buy film or pay for expensive processing, had been one of the wonders that Paul had introduced him to. Now, he had a phone with a good camera as well and he used whichever was available to capture pictures of animals, insects, and birds that he could use later for his drawings. He'd experimented with manipulating the photos with software, but he could never get the pictures that he wanted and was only satisfied when he drew the composition on paper and hand coloured it.

His drawings for Doreen Cattermole's children's stories had been accepted by the publisher and he'd agreed to try out three books, although it would be some time before they were in the shops, such was the way publishing worked.

Having involuntarily dipped his toe in the publishing process, Joseph T. Dene set up a simple website, with a lot of help from Paul, where he could showcase his nature drawings and a couple of discarded children's illustrations. It had been a suggestion from the publisher that prompted him to think about a book of his drawings and observations from his time on the road. His favourite sketch was from a night spent in a barn when he witnessed a stand-off between the farm cat and a fox for the pick of the barn's mice.

During that café test of her feelings, Diane had been surprised at the change in his confidence since the rather artificial atmosphere at Christmas. His description of a busy life of which she had no part, had upset her more than she felt it should. Having been physically abandoned by him once, she now worried that he was emotionally growing into a different person, and her increasing trust in him would not lead to anything but an acceptance of continuing their individual lives.

But wasn't that the best she'd ever hoped for since that devastating night at the wedding? The café meeting had left her confused and angry with herself. She'd turned down marriage to a kind and thoughtful companion for all the right reasons, at the time. And she'd needed time to get over the shock. But had a secret part of her wanted something more from a man who had started as loser Joss, but worked so hard to re-invent the Joseph she had once loved?

They walked through the flats, admiring the way the builders had kept the features and integrated them into modern fittings and technology.

'Don't you want your flat done up, Joseph, these are so lovely?'

'Not at all, I did get them to put in a few more electrical sockets for all the computer stuff, but it was comfortable as Dot left it and I can keep it clean and tidy, and it feels like she's still here, just waiting to pop out and start a good argument about modern youth or the parlous state of television programmes.'

As they went round, he described his duties as resident caretaker, doing minor repairs, keeping the front steps and railings looking smart and, of course, his pride and joy: the garden. Walking round, Joseph pointed out all the new planting that would come into riotous colour from spring onwards. To Diane he sounded like the proud father that had once played with Anne and told the world about her happy and talented future.

When she shivered slightly, he apologised for keeping her out for so long in the January cold and guided her out of the side gate and back up into the house where he'd prepared a homemade hot soup with fresh rolls collected from an artisan baker half an hour before she arrived. The baker had also supplied a quiche to which he added a green salad, and he had a French apple tart in reserve in case Diane stayed on and they had a snack mid-afternoon.

Naturally, most of their talk was about Anne, Rhys, and the coming baby. Diane had been thinking about how well they'd got on with Rhys's parents, Bill and Jane, and how on earth they could get together as a foursome before the baby was born.

'Joseph, I've been thinking about what support Anne will need when Rhys goes back to work, and she has the baby and the Park to deal with on her own. I know Bill and Jane will be around, but I want to help out as well and I expect you will too. Rather than leave it to chance what do you feel about meeting up with Bill and Jane to discuss what we can all offer in the way of time and transport?'

Clearly this was a new idea, and Joseph immediately saw the snag, choosing where to meet, his place or hers. He'd more room for socialising, but he wasn't confident to produce a full meal for four. Diane's flat was a bit cramped, but she was a good cook. Or they could all go out for a meal, but then he'd have to rely on Diane for transport.

He guessed she'd already worked out these scenarios, so had she also come up with an answer?

'Great idea. I like both, really down to earth and look how they pitched in at the café when needed. We could work out how it could be done, even if we don't know when we would be needed. I'm a bit stuck with not having transport, but I'm closer than any of you to Anne's house so I could easily get a taxi.

'Which still leaves how do we meet them to talk all this over? You have obviously had time to think about it, so what do you suggest?'

'Come on, Joseph don't leave it all to me. Maybe you've come up with something I haven't thought of.'

So, Joseph was forced to outline the three possibilities, his place, her place or restaurant, and their problems.

'There is another solution, but it may not be one that you would want to do, Diane. You could cook a meal here and there would be room to eat and sit around comfortably afterwards. But would you find that too big a step and imply that we were a couple, which we clearly aren't?'

If it was a solution that Diane had considered, she gave no sign. But now that he had brought it up.

'No, we are nowhere near being a couple, and I am still going to concerts and plays with Alistair. Although not in the same way.' She added. 'I think everybody recognises that. We can meet, like today and at Christmas, without rowing in public, or creating a difficult atmosphere. We have moved beyond that, but it doesn't mean we are a couple in any sense of the word, and I think Bill and Jane understand that.

'If that is your suggestion, then I would be OK with it. But could we have a practice so that I can get used to your cooker and find where everything is in the kitchen?'

By which, Joseph understood the outcome was exactly what Diane was anticipating.

The afternoon was spent talking through the possible arrangements, consuming coffee and the French apple tart, and Diane phoning Jane to discuss possible dates.

After which she phoned Anne and explained that the four of them were having a meal together to get to know one another better, as things had been difficult in the past.

'So, things are not difficult now, Mum?' Anne suspected there was more to this phone call than had been said so far.

'Well, it was a little difficult to arrange, as you know my place isn't very big for a dinner party ...'

'A dinner party?'

'Well, just the four of us. As I said, my place isn't big enough, and your dad's is big enough, but he couldn't cook a full meal, so we compromised.'

'You are going to cook the meal at Dad's? Wow, that's

a turn up for the books. Where are you now, by the way? I thought you were only popping in to see the new flats with Dad. Are you still there?'

'Well, there has been a lot to discuss, and he did me a lovely little lunch, and then, as the afternoon went on, we had a French apple tart with the coffee.'

'So, you are still there?' Anne was waving for Rhys to join her, and mouthing, 'Mum has been at Dad's all afternoon. Still there.'

Rhys laughed, 'Do you think he's cooking breakfast?'

'Shut up! No not you Mum. It's the dog barking.' Mouthing, 'This is important' before stifling a giggle.

'I can't hear the dog, Anne, but you can tell Rhys he'll get a clip round the ear when I see him next.'

The phone went dead.

'Oh, sugar. Do you think I really have offended her?' Rhys was contrite but looked up and realised that Anne was doubled over holding her stomach. His arm was round her and worry flooded his face, until she looked up and grinned. 'I don't know about upsetting Mum, but you certainly had an effect on this little one. I'll be black and blue inside if it kicks again like that.'

'What do you think? Is it 'Goodbye, Alistair'?'

'I don't know about Alistair, but Mum won't rush into anything with Dad yet. And, truthfully, I'm not sure Dad is that keen on a reconciliation as man and wife. He wants to make up for all the hurt he caused Mum, but, for the first time in his life he has a chance of making a career out of the things he loves doing, gardening, and drawing. He's fifty-nine and maybe he sees a new life rather than retirement, and would he be able to pursue it if he had the obligations of being a couple?'

'Hell, Anne, I hadn't thought of it that way. I just assumed that he would want to get back together as his ultimate goal. So, you think your mum is keener than him?'

'Not necessarily, but I think it has come as a shock that he may not be. And I'll tell you another thing, there is more to this meeting with your mum and dad than a 'getting to know you' session. They have met enough times at the Park and then at Christmas to know they get on well. They are up to something. And if you hadn't blown it, I would have found out.

'I think I might phone Samuel in the morning and arrange to see him about Dot. And, while I'm there I might pop in and see Dad. He will be easier to get round than Mum.'

'I always said you were a crafty moo; I can see where you got it from.'

22 Countdown to Baby

Having convinced Rhys and Gerry that her plans for the Park were based on a sensible assessment of the future and received the news that Gerry had found a way to "regularise" the finances to pay both Paul and Joss, all Anne had to do was convince the team at the Park.

George was the first person she needed on side, as he would see his worker, Paul, not only taken away from his gardening team for about half the week, but also to be promoted over him in Park policy matters. It was lucky that the discussion about Dot's baby had taken place, and the reassurance that Anne had given him about his importance was fresh in his mind. Not that he was totally surprised at Paul being given the increased responsibility, what with his background of a business degree and his knowledge of internet marketing. And Rhys and Anne would still be requiring weekly reports from both, so any disagreements could be ironed out during the phone call. Anne had drawn up clear lines of responsibility and added Joss to make up some of Paul's outside work.

Joss had jumped at the chance to be at the Park for longer hours. Filling in at weekends so the lads could have time off was all very well, but he missed the companionship of the daily routine and banter when they were all together for their break.

Next on Anne's list was Paul, and here she stepped delicately between giving him the impression that he had wide latitude to make decisions and having to refer them all to her for approval. Mr Silk had tidied up her contract idea and Gerry had set limits on income and how much Paul was authorised to spend on behalf of the Park. The contract was designed to run for six months starting in March, after which he would resume his original contract, with an uplift in salary, unless the Park wanted him to continue in post, in which case a new contract would be negotiated.

Anne and Rhys had spent hours working out scenarios if Paul should want to run his own business, and they decided the contract offered them a period of certainty for their most risky time, while making it easy for him to continue, if that is what they both wanted. The other risk factor was Mia. Her contract officially ran out at Christmas, but she was still coming in during the week to keep the café open for a few hours each day and allow Anne to work on all the changes. The café takings didn't cover her costs, but they decided that it was a service they had to keep open for the Park users, and the alternative of Anne running it was no longer an option.

More worryingly for Anne was the possibility of Mia influencing Paul to argue the contract or hand in his notice and start his own business straight away. What she and Rhys had decided was to infer that the contract was a great opportunity for Paul to see the realities of how a small business was run, rather than the theory taught for his college degree, which assumed graduates working in companies with a turnover measured in millions of pounds.

Happily, either Paul and Mia had realised he was not ready to go it alone, or he relished the twin challenges of running the Park and guiding it to be a ground-breaking ecological venue for the entire UK parks community. Either way, Anne's interview with him went swimmingly, once he came round to the idea of a fixed term contract, but with the guarantee of his old job back afterwards with increased pay.

Which just left Robin, whose job description wouldn't really change, but with the offer of the Park paying for him to do an online course on sustainable development and be part of the team taking the Park in its new direction.

Having secured all the staff agreement to the new arrangements and ideas, the next stage was to act quickly to make sure weird rumours didn't start circulating among the Park users. Prime among these, and the most likely to generate ten versions of any piece of gossip, were the Park Mothers, an amorphous group originally encouraged by Dot with a view to telling them what was going to happen. The group soon dismissed that idea, and some very outspoken opinions were expressed on both sides, before it settled down to becoming an informal, occasional meeting where each idea for the Park could be discussed, even though Dot had the final word.

When he took over, Rhys had stopped the meetings as he was too busy with his job to sit down and go through all the niggles and gripes. Instead, he relied on George to keep him informed and called a meeting if there was a genuine problem or he wanted to change things.

Anne, being at the Park every day, found the constant interruptions by individual Park users a distraction, and formalised the meetings again, but now included the footballers, model boat club, tennis players and others. This enabled her to stop the individual approaches when she was working, by telling people to get it on the agenda at the next meeting. The Park Mothers had taken to technology during the winter months and had a lively WhatsApp group, which Anne had declined to join, foreseeing the inevitable little personal disputes that could arise, and not wanting to be dragged in as some sort of arbiter. On the other hand, she could ask them to circulate a message about changes or events at the Park, and she had found it a surprisingly effective way of getting announcements into the local paper, without the lottery of press releases. Someone in the group obviously had the ear of a reporter, she didn't enquire too deeply in case it was pillow talk.

Now, it would be a way of getting over the changes of staff responsibilities and publicise the idea behind moving the Park towards a green agenda, without the rumour mill getting there first.

The reaction was immediate, and almost entirely negative. Change, Anne discovered, was BAD. A bit shocked by this reaction, and foreseeing the weekly newspaper being on the phone to her at once, as they loved a good dispute, she phoned Rhys, "somewhere in the Midlands", to discussed damage limitation. Only to discover that he thought the situation was a wonderful opportunity.

'Look at it this way, we believe in this change of direction, which not only has the support of the staff, but was proposed by them, so we have a great story to tell as the world wakes up to the need for taking the environment seriously. Deforestation in the Amazon, plastic waste clogging the seas, the hole in the ozone layer, the frightening extremes of weather, all these are BAD. We are only a tiny organisation, but we are determined to do our bit to make the world a cleaner and safer place for our children and their children, and that is GOOD.

'Can you call a meeting of the Park users for Friday afternoon? And you, me and the whole team will be there with facts, but more importantly, passionate arguments for our ideas, and we will win them over and have them as our greatest advocates before next week's paper comes out.'

The café was packed, standing room only, with Mia dodging between waving arms to hand out hot mugs of tea, no plastic or paper cups to be seen. Rhys welcomed everybody and explained how the ideas had come about and his pride in the staff, who had such a deep understanding of how the natural world was all connected, and the difference that could be made even here, in Chip Notting. He was followed by a surprise speaker, Councillor Robert Broome who congratulated the Park on all the work it did in the community, reminding them of the Christmas lights and the television given to the hospice. Then he expanded on the leading role that Chip Notting could hold in the development and history of environmental thinking. A bit over the top, but it went down well.

The last to speak was Anne, who brought the group nearly to tears with her vision for a cleaner and healthier future for her child, (touching the Bump), and their children.

Carefully choreographed by Rhys, she asked for their support as she looked forward to becoming a mother, and her child growing up proud of the Park.

Crashing applause, handkerchiefs abundant, the meeting ended with local reporter being invited in to interview the audience along with Rhys and Anne, who posed for photos with Anne holding the Bump and Rhys with adoring look.

Front page and two inside pages of photos and congratulatory quotes from local climate activists, Rhys was "well pleased", as they say in Essex.

Which was fine but left the problem that nothing had actually changed in the Park at all, and it wouldn't be long before this was noticed. Paul set Joss to work with the tractor to dig a trench around the places where there were bare railings, ready to plant new hedging for the small bird and animal cover. This provided a noisy and visual impact for the reporter and the Park Mothers, who would soon move on to other interests and not notice when little more happened for a couple of months. Rhys had been careful not to mention that it was likely to be five growing seasons before the full benefits would become obvious.

Two months to "Bump reveal", as Anne called it, and the house smelt of fresh paint. Large boxes were stacked in the spare room, containing the contents of a small house, cot, table, nursing chair, bottle sanitisers, baby alarm, mobiles, wardrobe, and cupboards, (flat packed). There was also a single box of disposable nappies, for travel and emergencies, as Anne was determined to use washable products, and avoid the production and landfill disaster that disposables had proved to be.

The baby seat was fitted in Anne's car and anchor points located in the motorhome, while Rhys discreetly checked his new company car would be properly equipped. Frequent phone calls and Skype conferences were had with Brenda and Dean, to make sure nothing was missed in the roll call of a modern baby's needs. The only thing they wouldn't have delivered was the hi-tech pushchair, as for all her modern ideas, Anne stuck to the belief that it was unlucky to have it in the house before the baby was born.

Both sets of parents were keen to offer advice, but much of the technology was new to them, and the necessity for a quality sound system in the nursery had them flummoxed. The evening when they were due to discuss what help they could offer the young couple was coming up fast, and Diane had shopped for two in preparation for testing out the kitchen at Joseph's flat.

'Twice in a month.' Mused Anne. 'Something's up.'

The dog, her only listener, heard "up" and obediently sat up, assuming it must be time for a walk, although Anne had noticed that almost anything she said could be a trigger for him to demand a walk. Perhaps it was true that animals could sense a change coming and so this might be attention seeking. She hoped there wouldn't be a problem when the baby was born, certainly there had been no sign of aggression with Brenda's baby. In fact, no reaction at all, Jem had just wandered off to his favourite spot in the garden and gone to sleep.

On the other hand, the baby might be a danger to the dog. He was getting on now, and a baby crawling up to him and wanting to play, pulling his hair, or thumping him on the nose with a toy, might not be meant spitefully, but the dog wouldn't know that.

Eight weeks to go, if the baby had listened obediently to the midwife.

23 The Parents Secretly Scheme

The kitchen in Joseph's flat was small, Dot had mostly just cooked for herself and would have met at a restaurant rather than cook for others. So, not only was it small, but it lacked the multiple accessories found in a normal kitchen, such as more than two saucepans, various shaped knives, more than one oven dish, jugs, spatulas and many, many other essentials for a dinner party.

Diane arrived in the afternoon with the ingredients, did an inventory, cursed Dot, and drove home to pick up a box full of equipment. By which time she got caught in the commuter traffic leaving London, arriving flustered and annoyed with herself for being in such a state in front of Joseph.

'It's alright for you, I have to do all the cooking and still sit down and pretend to be fresh as a daisy ...'

At which point she walked into the dining room and saw the immaculately ironed white tablecloth, with polished knives and forks, sparkling wine glasses and a huge bunch of flowers, definitely shop bought, carefully arranged in the one and only vase.

'I thought I had better make sure nothing else was missing, and this way I could see it all.'

'But the flowers, Joseph, they will wilt before Thursday.'

'Oh, they're for you, for going to so much trouble. I'll get some more for Thursday.'

The combination of anger with herself followed by this display of thoughtfulness, overwhelmed Diane, and she touched his hand and stood on tiptoe, as she used to do, and kissed him on the cheek.

Joseph stood in shock, for a moment too long, and Diane moved away to sort out the kitchen, with a quiet, 'It doesn't mean anything.' under her breath.

This spoiled rather than helped the cooking "practice", as she was on edge the whole time not to give the wrong signals, staying a little distance from him, and keeping up a constant bombardment of small talk. If Joseph was perplexed, he didn't show it, moving around her to put away all the special table layout, and substituting the ordinary cutlery and plates for the two of them.

Diane served up, complaining that the meat was overdone as the cooker was very fierce compared with hers. Joseph gently disagreed, saying it was perfectly cooked, as was everything, and they both knew that if it had been charcoal the same conversation would have taken place.

Joseph was first to break the conventions.

'Since I've been back in the normal world, as you might call it, I have learned a lot of new expressions. Like "elephant in the room", which had me completely lost for an explanation when I first heard it. But I think it describes what we are doing, Diane, we are ignoring the biggest question that we both know exists, but neither of us is willing to get out into the open. So, I'm going to ask it because it is screwing me up inside.'

Diane went to put her hand up to stop him, and then thought better of it.

'Do you think you will ever trust me again?'

Diane looked up from her previous detailed examination of her empty plate, set her elbows on the table, joined her hands, and started chewing the joint of her right thumb. Joseph knew that pose so well, and he began to regret his eagerness and stupidity.

'A year ago, the answer would have been "absolutely not, ever". I won't say I hated you, but I hated what you had put Anne and me through in all those years. You know this, I made my feelings quite clear after the wedding where you reappeared.

'Since then, I have watched you earn the respect of the people you work with and Anne. She would have loved you anyway, but respect must be earned. However, the defining one was Rhys. He had no reason to trust you whatever Anne's feelings were, he makes his own judgements, that's why he is so good at his job. He understands people, their motivations, their ambitions, their weaknesses. I gather he gave you, his father-in-law, a good talking to, one day about buying drink?

'Yes, I do know about that, Joseph. What I also know is that he trusts you as much as any of the other lads at the Park, which is saying a good deal.'

Here Diane stopped and nibbled her thumb for a few moments. If Joseph was breathing, it didn't show.

'I want to trust you, Joseph, and that is a tremendous change. And I believe you have turned your life round in an extraordinary way, helped by the people around you, not forgetting the remarkable Dot. But you are still an alcoholic, and I do understand that will never change, it is a demon you will have to fight all your life. Perhaps the question is not "will I ever trust you", but will I ever feel that I want to be part of your struggle?

'Because, we have too much history to be just friends. We can be acquaintances, like we are now, or more than friends, whatever that means. And I'm not sure what you want, you have been on your own for so long, making your own decisions, however bad, and now you are building your own busy life with a book illustrating career in the offing.

'Really, there have been two elephants in the room, and I'm not sure you have realised that.'

She was right. He wanted her forgiveness, but what then? The most he had dared hope for was friendship, but now this was being tugged away. Would he be satisfied with the relationship they had now, which she described as acquaintance? He became aware that Diane was looking increasingly anxious, waiting for his reaction.

'You are right, Diane, I haven't looked to the future, because I never dreamed we would ever have one. I thought it might become a more relaxed version of what we are now, without the constant tension of your suspicion that I might just disappear again. I called that friendship, but now you are saying that is not possible for us.

'What do I want? That has not even been in my dreams, because what we have now so far exceeds anything I ever hoped for when I first saw you visit the Park with Rhys and Anne. And it's not only me that has had a very different life for thirty years, but you have also had experiences I couldn't imagine. Anne said you took her to Paris. Paris. The only place I took you to was Brighton. I've never been abroad, never had a passport, never been in an aeroplane, never watched our child take her exams or go to university, have a first boyfriend. I haven't slept with someone for about fifteen years or driven a car for longer. You have done all those things, so we both have some catching up to do before we can become better than friends.

'I suppose, what I am trying to say, is that one day, I would like us to be a real family again, but I recognise there is a very long way to go, and perhaps we could start by just getting to know our new selves. I expect "courting" has long gone out of fashion, but that is what I think I would like to do. To go out on "dates". Does that sound weird? To get to know one another's tastes, find out what we can talk about and what is too raw at the moment.'

Joseph stuttered to a halt; it was probably the longest personal declaration he had made in those intervening thirty years.

'Joseph, that not only sounds weird, it is weird, but it's weird, nice. I think we could consider going to places, having meals out, that sort of thing, but I draw the line at going to the pictures so you can try and get your hand in my bra.'

Joseph looked horrified, 'No, no, I didn't mean anything like that!'

'You don't find me attractive anymore?'

'No, no. I mean yes …'

'OK. You can stop now; I was only winding you up. You always were gullible. Can you make me some coffee, I will have to drive home soon and it's a horrible night? Before you ask, that isn't a signal for you to invite me to stay the night while you sleep on the sofa. That is not going to happen.'

They both knew that making the coffee was a tactic for them to regroup. It had been a tremendous step in their relationship and they both needed a few minutes to decide the next move. Hovering in the background was the other elephant neither had wanted to talk about. Where did Alistair fit in?

With the coffee came agreement to meet again, after the dinner party with Rhys's parents. There was no kiss goodnight, just a friendly wave as she reached the car.

Happily married for nearly forty years, Bill and Jane were inclined to finish one another's sentences and anticipate each other's thought processes, so that changes of subject could have them both starting to tell the same anecdote together. It wasn't that they weren't individuals; their personalities were in many ways opposites. He was laid back and seldom flustered, while she tended to get aggravated or anxious if things didn't go to plan first time. They had rubbed together for so long and had the same experiences and talked about them to so many friends, that they appeared to be a single entity. Although they knew the history of Joseph and Diane and had met them at the Park and at Christmas, they still found the studied politeness between the two rather disconcerting. 'Neither fish nor fowl', as Jane put it, 'they're still married, but not a couple. She doesn't trust him not to run off again, and he goes to AA and lives in my sister's old house. Not that I begrudge him that, after all it was Rhys Dot left it to, Joseph is just a lodger. Dot and her husband must have done very well to leave me a tidy sum as well, enough for us to retire early. And we now know that she was supporting the Park at the end.'

They hadn't visited Dot at her house very often and they didn't stay the night after Rhys had nightmares the first time. Seeing the house turned into three flats was a revelation, with Joseph doing the guided tour. He hadn't changed much about Dot's own flat, that she had retreated to after her husband died. It had been papered, painted, and had a new carpet, but the layout and furniture remained as she would have recognised it.

Jane and Joseph talked about Dot, but it was like describing two different people, the first fairly conventional before the Park and the second outrageously campaigning for the community she had created. Jane and Bill had seen little of her once the Park took hold, but they had read plenty in the local newspaper that they had delivered by post to their home every week.

The meal went well, and Diane explained about the practice they had the week before and the lack of cooking utensils. This made Jane laugh as she explained that they never saw Dot cook a meal. Every time they were going to visit, Dot would insist on taking them all out to a restaurant, declaring she wasn't some overrated, and over made up, TV cook like Fanny Cradock, who had nothing else to do all day but play at being an ordinary housewife.

'Ordinary housewife?', Dot used to say, 'Harping on about how this wine goes with this dish, and that wine goes with that dish, when most ordinary housewives of the time only tasted wine at Christmas, in their festive port and lemon, while they did the washing up. Bloody hypocrite'.

When they finally got round to talking about how they could help with looking after the grandchild, when Anne went back to work at the Park, there was much discussion on where to look after him, or her. With Jane, Bill and Diane, living in North London, there would be a lot of commuting to pick up the baby in the morning and for Anne to collect in the evening. Unless they stayed at the baby's home for the day, where everything was available, cot, clothes, bath, and the myriad other needs of a tiny being. Plus, they could let the dog out into the garden, do the washing and ironing and put the dinner on, if necessary. Joseph insisted he could help if he wasn't working, and if Anne did what she said, and only worked four days a week, which would mean they only did one day a week each. Except that Bill and Jane said they would come over together on their days.

And so it was settled, but, like pushchairs, they didn't want to tempt fate by mentioning it to Anne and Rhys until after the baby was born.

Despite her intuition, Anne had to be satisfied with a bland account of the dinner party from her mum, although Rhys heard from his mum, how she was amazed at the warmth between Joseph and Diane since she last saw them at Christmas.

24 Two Emergencies!

A month to go, and there was a character swap between the parents, Anne became relaxed and serene, while Rhys was jumpy every time the phone went at work, kept his car full of petrol, checked the hospital bag twice a day and generally became a caricature of a first-time father.

Rhys, Anne, and Paul had gone through the handover details, looking at various possible emergency scenarios, and updating the Park's disaster recovery plan, covering everything from flood to drought, from electrical outages to staff illness. Not that Paul would be on his own for long. Rhys would have a month off, hard fought from the American parent company, so either he or Anne would be able to step in when Paul had his days off, if necessary. After that, Anne said she could take the baby with her if she needed to go to the Park for anything.

But March turned very cold, with snow showers and strong winds. Winters were never a good time for Joss, no matter how well fed, clothed, or housed, his time on the road had taken its toll. He phoned George to say he couldn't make it into work one morning, and he sounded so bad that George phoned Anne. Ignoring the midwife's advice to rest, even if she felt the need to clean the house, bath the dog or paint a wall, Anne rushed round to find Joss in a bad way, sweating and having difficulty breathing. For the first time in her life, she called 999 and within ten minutes an ambulance was outside. Another twenty minutes and Joss was getting the full ''blues and twos" treatment on the way to hospital, followed by a frantic Anne. She knew Rhys was in Birmingham that day, but the paramedics had mentioned pneumonia, so she had phoned her mum instead when she got to the hospital.

At which point her waters broke, two weeks early.

The nurse assured her that it was nothing to worry about, two weeks when the baby was as active as hers just meant it was itching to get out into the world to make its mark.

And, yes, she would find out what was happening to her father, but just let the doctors do their job, and concentrate on the next generation for a few minutes.

And, yes, she could phone her husband, and her mother, but not for the next couple of minutes while they had a listen and an examination.

Anne was completely lost. She had absolutely no control over what was going to happen to her, the baby, or her father. And her life support, her mobile phone, was forbidden until the nurses had finished her ''internal''. She wanted Rhys. She wanted her mum. She wanted to cry, or scream, or swear, anything to put her back in control.

'Well, it's all calmed down now.' The nurse was reassuring. 'It may have been the shock about your father that helped it along, but I'd guess you are a few hours off starting yet, but we will keep you in, you will probably want to be in the hospital anyway, so you might as well be comfortable, and we can keep an eye on things.'

Anne had her lifeline back, her mobile and a connection to Rhys.

'Ree, my waters have broken.'

'What? Two weeks early? OK, get a taxi, don't drive, phone your mum, I'll pick up the overnight bag later ...'

'Listen Ree, I'm OK, I'm at the hospital and they've

checked me over and they don't think I'll start for several hours. Please listen, stop interrupting. It happened in the hospital because they have just brought Dad in with suspected pneumonia. Shut up Ree and listen. Mum is on her way, although she doesn't know about me yet. So, this is an instruction, Ree. Drive very, very carefully. I'd rather the baby arrived before you got here, than arrived without a father. Be careful, Rhys Banks, and remember, I love you so much. Now get off the phone, make your excuses and drive carefully for the three of us.'

It was too late to phone her mum now, she would be on her way and didn't have hands free in her car. Anyway, now that things had a bit more perspective it probably wasn't a good idea to tell her mum that her waters had broken until she arrived, she didn't want another member of the family ending up in hospital. There was still no news about her dad, and all the nurses were very busy, Mum wouldn't be at the hospital for at least half an hour, so the canteen beckoned.

A quick phone call to George to tell him about Joss and get him to alert Paul that his new duties were starting immediately.

Then phone Bill and Jane so that they wouldn't feel left out.

But, what about the dog? They had always assumed Dad would see to him while they were at the hospital. The only other person who knew the dog well was Robin, who had built his kennel and his dog run. Another phone call to George, asking if he could get Robin to phone her. There was a house key in the Park safe for emergencies, and this was certainly an emergency.

Back down to Reception, just in time to see her mum come in, looking dreadful.

'How is he? Anne, you look ever so white; it must be the shock. Have they said anything?'

'Nothing so far, they were trying to get his temperature down, they said it might take some time.

'Sit down Mum, you don't look so good yourself. I have some other news, when I got here, my waters broke. They examined me and said it has calmed down and it might have been the shock with Dad. I haven't started, and it could be some time before I do. Rhys is on his way back from Birmingham, I've told him to drive very carefully, after all I'm in the best possible place.

'Mum, I think you need a strong cup of coffee, so come on, I know my way to the canteen.'

'Hold on, Mrs Banks, I wondered where you had got to, you're supposed to be resting.' The nurse was looking stern. 'And would this be your mother, Mrs Dene? I have some news about Mr Dene. This isn't the first time he has had pneumonia, although we haven't been able to locate the records yet. But you already know that, and the last time scarred his lungs which has caused some worry about his condition when we stabilise him. The doctor will be able to tell you more, but he is going to need careful looking after for at least a couple of weeks when he comes out, I take it that won't be a problem? I only ask as he has Mrs Banks down as his next of kin, not Mrs Dene, and clearly she will not be able to cope with him and the baby.'

Before Anne could reply, her mother answered. 'There won't be a problem, I will take care of him.'

'Good. Now Mrs Banks, no more gallivanting, I want to know where you are so we can keep an eye on you. I have arranged a relative's room with a bed for you, and your mum can organise food and drink, I'm sure. Someone from Gynae will be along to see you soon and they will arrange to take you up to the ward nearer your time.'

When Anne was settled on the bed and the nurse had

gone, she looked at her mum and asked the question that wouldn't go away.

'How, Mum? How are you going to look after him? You live in North London, and he lives in Chip Notting? We could get a nurse; you don't have to do it.'

'I know I don't have to do it, that's not the point. He is still my husband and, well, just lately we have been seeing more of each other, we even went to the pictures together. I wasn't going to tell you until things had calmed down. But I'm sure he is a good man at heart, and he has worked so hard to win everybody's trust, am I supposed to fail him when he needs me, even though he did that to me all those years ago?'

'Well, that's a shock. You and Dad going to the pictures. But, be practical Mum, he needs someone there all the time, there's only one bedroom and he will be in that. You can't sleep on the sofa every night, and what about your clothes, and what if he needs help with personal things?'

'I'm sure we can get some sort of temporary bed set up in the lounge and I can pop home for clothes before he comes out. As for "personal things" as you so delicately put it, I'm too old to worry about that, I've slept with four men, as you well know, including your father. That really isn't a problem.'

'Maybe not for you; what about Dad? How will he feel? A nurse is different, but you?'

'He'll just have to put up with it, all our attention will be on you and the baby, our grandchild. Have you thought of any names yet?'

'Don't change the subject, Mum. Ooooh! That was a kick, or something.'

Luckily, the nurse from Gynae arrived to do her checks, and shooe'd Diane out to the canteen.

On her way back, after anxiously counting to fifteen

minutes, she met the first nurse.

'Mrs Dene, I was looking for you. Your daughter has been taken up to the ward, nothing wrong, but these first births can be unpredictable, so they decided to have her close by. It wasn't your daughter I wanted to tell you about. Mr Dene has been moved to a side room where we are still trying to get his temperature down by having all the windows open. But he is much better, sitting up and able to have visitors. Do you want to see him now?'

Joss was visibly shocked to see her, he was still sweating profusely and had his pyjama jacket open, which he clenched together when she walked in.

'Where's Anne?'

'Anne is OK, did they tell you her waters broke in the waiting room, and she's now safely tucked up in the gynaecological ward, the best place for her.'

'Does Rhys know, he's in Birmingham?'

'He's on his way, everything is under control, and before you ask, George knows, Robin is looking after the dog and Paul is taking over at the Park. Now, what's all this about you having pneumonia before?'

'That was a long time ago, a bad winter, sleeping where I could, drinking, of course, and I ended up in hospital for about three weeks. They discharged me to a hostel with my own room and I had to attend hospital every day.'

He broke off to cough, which made him sweat more.

'But it didn't last, the hostel couldn't afford a room for a single person, and they put in a bunk bed for two others, one with mental problems and the other a druggie. I left and went back on the road, by then it was spring, and I got a job with a friendly farmer.'

He started coughing again and a nurse came in to check his temperature. 'Two minutes more and then I must ask you leave while he rests, Mrs Dene.'

'You will let me know about the baby, won't you? I want to be around to see our grandchild grow up, Diane.'

'Oh, I'm going to make sure you are.' And she reached for his hand and squeezed it hard.

25 It's a Boy!

Anne fidgeted in her NHS nightdress, insisting that she didn't need to get into bed, but couldn't get comfortable sitting on a chair either. She tried reading a novel on her phone, looked at the news, listened to some of Women's Hour, and fretted alternately about Rhys arriving safely, and her dad's reaction to being looked after by her Mum.

She knew she shouldn't ignore the spasms that were getting slowly more insistent, but Diane returned, took one look at her, and called a nurse. In no uncertain terms, the nurse pointed out that the baby was unaware of the state of the motorways and would pop out when they felt it was time, not wait for the father to arrive, however much wriggling Anne might do.

When Diane finally confessed that she hadn't told Joss that she would be looking after him, Anne started thinking about alternatives again. Which at least took her mind off the time she was so familiar with counting down, as Rhys always phoned her as he left or passed Birmingham, "on the home run" as he put it. He had phoned when he was still about an hour away, but Anne told him that nothing was happening and to just concentrate on arriving safely.

By the time nature had decided time was up, and Diane had been shocked at her daughter's facility with swearing, under the influence of gas and air, Rhys had arrived. Expecting to be waiting around but walking into the final fifteen minutes of a calm but busy delivery, he was hustled into protective clothing, and thrust into a situation even the most explicit video couldn't prepare him for. The emotional impact could never be conveyed by even the most lyrical presenter, and Rhys was tearfully overwhelmed, holding their baby for the first time. Anne looked on and wondered aloud which boy was going to give her more trouble.

The baby boy entered the world nameless, as the parents hadn't been able to agree on a male name, although a girl would have been Theia, a modern version of Dorothy. There were more tears of relief and joy, hugs and proud Diane rushed off to tell Joss the good news.

After a period of Ooohing and Ahhhing, and noises only a baby was supposed to understand, the little human dropped off to sleep, and Rhys remembered to ask how Joss was.

The story of his recovery, the secret cinema visit and the bombshell that Diane was going to move into Joss's flat to look after him, left an already emotionally drained Rhys, completely speechless. After a few moments, Anne looked at him and diagnosed the problem.

'You didn't stop for an iced bun sugar rush and a coffee, did you?'

'Of course not. What do you mean, Diane is moving in with your dad, how will that work? What did he say?'

'I don't know how it will work and she hasn't told Dad yet. I did suggest we could get a nurse in, but she won't have it. Now, new daddy, get yourself to the canteen and eat that horribly fattening sticky bun, washed down with a strong coffee, I'm not going anywhere for a while. Well, probably another two or three hours before they chuck me and 'im out. Oh, and think about Oliver or Kieran.'

Rhys found the canteen, and a jolly lady with Marjory sewn onto her overall. One look at him, and the bun, and the black coffee.

'Boy or girl?'

'Err, boy.'

'No name yet then?'

'Err, no.'

'Thought not, new dads can't wait to tell someone if they've chosen a name. Must be your first, still looking shell shocked. Take my advice, have two buns, you'll need the energy in the next twenty-four hours.'

'Thanks, how did you know? You must get people from all over the hospital in here.'

'Oh, you soon get to tell. A mixture of walking in a dream somewhere above the floor, with eyes wider than normal, but seeing nothing. Some of them don't make it to the counter, they collapse in the nearest chair. Sometimes we notice they are still sat there half an hour later, and we have to go over and remind them to have a cup of tea and get back downstairs before the wife thinks they've run off. I think you had better take your buns and tea and find a table before you pass out.'

'Thanks, it was a long drive, I was in Birmingham. What do you think, Oliver or Kieran?'

'Take my advice, have 'em both. No regrets and they're both good names if he wants to swap them around later.'

Two eaten, but untasted, iced Belgian buns and a lukewarm coffee later, and a call to his very excited parents, he was back with Anne and Oliver Kieran Banks.

'You know he could end up being called OK, don't you? But I've heard a lot worse nicknames.' Anne was recovered, and "OK" was having his first feed. 'Come on, get your phone out and take some beautiful pictures, just for us. Then I'll cover up a bit and you can take some for everybody else. Mum popped in to have a cuddle with him, and me, but mostly him. Apparently, she told Dad her plans for looking after him, and he said no. No way was he going to have her giving up her independence and taking on an invalid.

'Mum can be straight talking sometimes, probably where I got it from, before you say it. Anyway, ignoring all the other patients and visitors, she announced that she had slept with him more times than she cared to remember, washed his pants as many times, and cleaned up his sick when he was drunk, so helping him to dress, feed him and chucking his clothes in the washing machine was hardly life changing. Then one of the other patients piped up and declared he was bloody lucky to have her, he wished his wife was still alive to look after him.

'I think Dad knew when he was beaten, so she's off home to get some things ready to move in as soon as he can be discharged. Talking of which, you have about an hour to get home, pick up my bag and get back here with a nice warm car to take your family home for a first night of little sleep.'

26 Paul in Charge

When Paul saw George hurrying over to where he was marking out the display plan in a flower bed, he thought he had picked up the wrong design. The news that he was starting his new responsibilities immediately, left him stunned. No matter how many times he had gone through the details with Anne, and Rhys, and George, and Mia, now it was his responsibility, he was numb. The idea that the whole Park project was down to him, while not being strictly the case, was enough to make his shoulders sag with the weight, that he realised was much heavier for Anne and Rhys.

But this was the great opportunity he and Mia had discussed, to learn about the realities of running a small business, to drive forward the green potential of the Park, to promote his own name in the journals and magazines that would matter when he started his own business, their own business. He reached for his phone, and then remembered George was waiting for him to say something.

'Wow. I hope Anne is OK. And Joss. What are we going to do without Joss?'

And there it was, his first decision and he was asking George. His brain sparked back into action.

'Right, George, I have a mate whose son is at agricultural college in Hertfordshire. He wants a weekend job so we could try him out. And, if he's any good, he can work over the Easter holidays if we need more help. Not a long-term solution, but we don't know when Joss will be back, if at all. We'll have to tackle that when we know for sure.'

George nodded and smiled. He was sure Paul could handle the responsibility; his only concern was Mia's ambition.

Mia had a more urgent take on the situation.

'I can manage in the café for now, as we agreed, but I'll have to start sounding out staff for Easter and beyond. Obviously, Anne or Rhys will do the final interview, but I want to find someone who can handle the Park Mothers as well as do the job. They can be very intimidating if you're not careful. Always after that extra biscuit or biggest slice of cake. When I started, Anne warned me and made it clear to them that she wasn't having any nonsense. I suppose I will have to do the same with a new girl.'

Paul hadn't really considered this part of his new responsibilities.

'Why girl? Have you thought about a male catering student, that might give them something to think about.'

Realising, too late, that this might be not such a great idea. 'Although, I'm sure you could handle any problems with a girl or boy.'

'Oh, no! The Park Mothers would be even worse with a young lad from college, they'd be flirting, embarrassing him, I wouldn't put it past one or two of them to pinch his bum. No, no, a girl it must be with that lot. I bet you had one or two invitations, didn't you? All those muscles on display when you were digging the flower beds or playing football at the weekends.

Paul reddened under his tan, remembering the day he had rescued that little sod, Arnie, from the lake. And the circle of Mothers clapping, with wolf whistles and cries of 'Ohhh, Mr Darcy.'

Mia watched and guessed. 'But, of course, you are

experienced enough to handle it, I doubt if a seventeen-year-old would realise the consequences of getting involved with a Park Mum with a two-year-old and a partner away on long distance lorries. And I'm damned sure Rhys or Anne would see it as my fault. So, no college hunks, thank you very much.'

'Wow. Listen to you, in two minutes you have matured by ten years and started your own little business with one employee.'

'Best I practise here, before we start our own little business.'

27 Two New Households

The first few days and nights fully lived up to the expectations of parenthood. Days when feeding, nappy changes, washing nappies and baby clothes, snatching a couple of hours relaxation, interrupted by a parental visit, phone calls, Skype calls to relatives and friends, all merged into an exhilarated numbness.

Just when the first day was drifting into evening, New York woke up, and "that bloody man", Rhys's boss alerted everybody in Head Office to the new arrival. At which point the message page lit up with requests for pictures and animated congratulations cards.

Anne tried to get Rhys to get some sleep at night, she was feeding Oliver, so he didn't need to worry about heating and cleaning bottles. But Rhys insisted that she was as tired as he was and might drop off to sleep, so he would keep her company. By morning a screaming son woke them to the horrified thought that they were already failing parents and their poor child's future was doomed through neglect in his first week of life.

'Who would have believed we would be relying on Brenda and Dean to mentor us', said Anne. 'I remember some of the mothers at ante-natal saying that you had to get your own sleep even if it meant the baby woke up first. But I was determined that we would never do that. So, I was dreading telling Brenda and Dean that we had overslept, and then they just laughed and said everybody did, babies are very resilient. And they were right, we don't know if he had just started screaming and we woke up straight away, but perhaps it is no bad thing that he doesn't think he is in control with us running at his first scream. I read somewhere that babies are born as intelligent as adults, they just lack experience. So, perhaps Brenda is right, little nipper is trying to control us.'

'Like in The Exorcist you mean? I don't think we will have to endure a spinning head and projectile vomiting, well not the spinning head at least.'

'I don't know what you are talking about, was it a film? Is that what you got up to before I took you in hand, going to horror movies about Devil babies? I don't want to know any more Ree. Take the dog for a walk and clear your head, and I'll make sure I don't upset young Oliver.'

Grandparents Bill and Jane came and "Ooooooh'd" with the baby. Grandparent Diane came and ''Aaaaaah'd" with the baby. Brenda popped in and talked baby talk with the baby, with lots of funny faces and waving of hands. While the parents sat back and had an uninterrupted cup of tea.

Cards crowded every horizontal space, including an enormous one, signed by all the Park Mums, with a PS asking when Anne would be taking Oliver to meet them.

By day three the sun came out and the buggy was proudly set up in all its Formulae One inspired glory and pushed all of twenty feet out into the garden. The sunshade was tweaked, the covers adjusted, the insect netting arranged. And the new parents discovered the one fact that had not been disclosed by anybody. Babies will sleep for hours in the fresh air. Anxious parents checking to see if he was still breathing after two hours, then three, then four. Phone calls to Brenda, and parents, to discover that everyone knew about this phenomenon, and had assumed the whole world was aware of this fact of life.

What a difference it made as the sun shone over the

next few days. Rhys insisted on another bit of technology, a baby alert attached to the buggy that triggered their mobile phones if the baby cried. The camera already covering the garden added to their peace of mind as that gave yet another ringtone if anything moved. The dog was kept inside unless they were out in the garden. Not that he had shown the slightest interest in either the baby or the buggy, but he did like all the company during the day and the frequent attention from visitors.

Joss was discharged from hospital into Diane's care and told to rest for at least a week. But it was not in his nature to sit around so, each time Diane returned from seeing the baby, there would be some little sandwiches or muffins to accompany her cup of tea.

Now he had access to the computer he saw the baby for the first time via a Skype call and it drew tears in his weakened state. A day he could never have imagined just a year ago.

Neither could he have imagined having Diane living under the same roof and looking after him. It was very difficult for both of them at first. Stupid things, like when to turn the television on, then what to watch.

'You choose.'

'No, it's your home, you decide.'

'I only watch the News, and some of the documentaries. Sometimes the old comedy shows, I've missed so much with all those years on the road, that I never run out of things to see. So, whatever you choose will be new and interesting.'

'Like knitting?'

'I learned to knit one time when I was on the wagon for a while. Had a good job on a farm and the farmer, an old boy, was on his own. His wife had taught him to knit, and he taught me. Very companionable activity is knitting, and I made a thick jersey before I fell off the wagon and had to leave. But that jersey kept me warm for three winters, so I wouldn't mind seeing a knitting programme.'

'I was only joking. You are a dark horse. Drawing and now knitting, what else did you learn on your travels?'

Joss noted that his demeaning time as a drunken tramp was being morphed into "his travels" and smiled inwardly.

The evening passed without the television being switched on, him talking more in a few hours than he had done in a whole week during the nearly thirty years on "his travels".

He had insisted that the only way he would consent to her staying was that she had the bedroom, and he would sleep on a camp bed that Paul had loaned him, in the main room. They parted with a formal, 'Good night.'

Always an early riser, it meant he could be up, have his shower and clear the bed away before she woke. He had gathered the last of the daffodils from the garden into a display on the breakfast table by the time Diane appeared, fully dressed after a fitful night's sleep. She was cross with herself for allowing him to get breakfast when she should have been making sure he rested. But he was in such good spirits that she decided to make sure he didn't do anything else for the rest of the day.

However, she had not allowed for the phone calls, Anne, George, Paul, Robin, Bill and Jane, Dennis the ice cream man, even Doreen Cattermole.

Then the doorbell went.

Samuel stood there looking distraught, and with a big bunch of flowers in his hand.

'Hello, we almost met the other day, I'm Samuel in case you have forgotten, and you must be … Joss's ex-wife, I'm guessing?'

'Wife.'

'Oh, sorry. I didn't know.'

'Obviously.' She smiled at his confusion.

'Well, I was coming round to give Joss some flowers to pass on to Anne and Rhys for their new baby. But when I spoke to Paul at the Park, he said Joss was in hospital. Then I saw your car here, all night, and I thought, "Not good news, I thought." So, how is Joss?' Trying to get all that out without taking a breath, and obviously embarrassed, he steadied himself on the stair rail.

Diane took pity on him. 'Are you alright, Samuel? At the moment you look worse than Joseph. He is supposed to be resting now otherwise I would invite you in.'

Samuel retrieved his breathing, renewed his natural smile, and let go of the handrail. 'So, he's alright then, nothing serious?'

'Well, pneumonia for the second time can be pretty serious, but with rest he should be a lot better in a couple of weeks. Shall I take the flowers? I will be going to see Anne this afternoon for a short visit. I'll tell Joseph you called, and thank you Samuel.'

28 Crisis Management

The Spring Show was the highlight of the inter-park rivalry across the district. Last year Ladywood Park had won both categories, best display, and most community involvement. This year the changes needed to reconfigure the Park into an environmental haven ruled out the usual massed floral displays. They had planted some formal flower beds to balance the areas that were going to be wildflower sites in a year or so's time. But there was no attempt to enter the display category this year. Then there was the new pathway, wriggling its way from the car park to the children's play area. Roughly dug out and with young trees being planted either side along its length, the path would be a wooden walkway sourced from sustainable forests and enable wheelchair users to access most of the Park even when the ground was wet. The cost had been enormous, but Councillor Broome had discovered that the Community Grants Officer at the Council was expert at writing proposals for extracting money from numerous obscure Government bodies. He did this on behalf of all sorts of local voluntary organisations, but his real interest was in environmental issues. An introduction to avid campaigner, Robin with his ideas for a miniature forest, but spaced out rather than in a clump, soon had him intrigued, then enthusiastic. Much paperwork, hopefully all reused, and many inspections followed before funds from myriad sources started to flow and trees could be ordered.

While Joss had been around, and Paul was full time on

the planting it had not been a problem to release Robin to oversee the project. But now, with the path still a mud bath after all the rain, and more trees to be delivered and planted, Robin was needed for all the other Park essentials, including an extensive outreach programme with local schools. Normally, Mia helped Robin with the preparation, designing the graphics and printing off all the quiz sheets in between helping Anne in the café. Now she was running it full time and taking on a temporary assistant, there was no time for the schools' projects. And Robin couldn't cope.

The new part-time gardener was interviewed by George and turned out to be a useful addition, and vital so that everybody could get their days off at the weekends. But it still left George taking over organising the tree planting and liaising with groups interested in the green project and leaving later and later as he attempted to print all the school sheets and itineraries that Robin couldn't manage.

Paul and Anne had spent a long time going through the workload that she was expecting him to do while she was away, but nothing had quite prepared him for the flood of paperwork that arrived every day. Anne had been doing it for so long that much of it she binned on the basis that, were it really important, they would write again. Paul couldn't do that and so spent much of his time researching ideas and projects that were ultimately going nowhere. This ate into the time he should have been working on the gardens, thus adding to George's problems.

It all came to a head when a school party was due, and there was no paperwork ready, a lorry load of trees turned up a day early, Paul was in a meeting with the engineers installing the new electric charging points and Mia had two candidates for café assistant to interview.

Robin was complaining to George. George was phoning the tree company and discovering that they had emailed the Park about the changed delivery, but Paul had never passed the message on. Paul wanted Robin to drive the tractor to dig the trench for the new cables, but George needed the tractor to dig the holes for the trees. And Mia wanted Paul to sit in on one of the interviews to confirm that the candidate was suitable to be recommended to Anne and Rhys.

It was, of course, raining. Robin wanted his school group in the café where they had an overhead projector and screen for such weather, but that was where Mia was interviewing.

Sipping his fourth cup of tea since the early hours, Rhys put the local paper on one side and surveyed the carnage that preceded the morning sleep for the baby. Anne was still in her pyjamas and had her feet up on the settee, a healthy glass of some khaki-coloured liquid half drunk on the table beside her.

'I'll clear up while you take the dog for a walk.'

Rhys glanced out of the window. 'Sure you wouldn't like some fresh air?'

'You're dressed, put a coat on and don't be a ninny. But you had better do your daily call to George first.'

It took about five seconds before Rhys heard the strife in George's voice and asked what was going on.

As the jigsaw jumble of problems clattered on his sleep-deprived brain, Rhys reminded himself he was a director of a large company. All this needed was fifteen minutes of careful analysis, and a coffee. Neither were available.

'No problem,' he heard himself say. Well, that was his first problem, obviously his mouth wasn't attached to his brain. Think! What is most urgent? The school trip, already on their way.

'Tell Mia to do her interview in the office and I will be over to join her soon. That will free up the café for Robin with the school party.'

'What about Paul, who is in the office with the engineers?'

'He will have to go downstairs to the storeroom and sit on a sack, that or use the football changing rooms. Which leaves the tractor, the cable trench can wait, the trees can't. I'm afraid you will have to handle that, George.

'After I have finished the interview with Mia, I want a meeting with you and Paul to find out what went wrong and how you will both avoid it happening again.'

Anne was looking very concerned when he came off the phone.

'I was supposed to have managed the Park, so this never had to involve you, I'm sorry Ree. Can I do anything from here?'

Rhys was putting on his coat and apologising to the dog, who was already at the door, tail wagging furiously.

'I think we need to find out where the system broke down first. Your plan looked perfectly fine to me. Did someone not follow the plan or is the plan the problem? That's what I will find out.

'Will you be alright on your own with Oliver? It will be the first time.'

'Don't be daft, of course I can cope, just go, and watch out for Mia's beam.'

The café assistant interview went well, although it may not have done if Rhys had known that the girl had asked Mia whether he was married.

The sun came out and Robin managed to get some time outdoors with his school party. Even the mud was less daunting to George digging holes for the new trees.

Paul was nowhere to be seen.

Rhys had a coffee and an iced bun in the café as a reward, and phoned Anne to check on Oliver, who he hadn't seen for nearly two hours. He discussed the lack of students notes with Robin and Mia and could see that they were both overstretched, which would be relieved when the new girl started, but should not have reached that stage without alarm bells ringing. He could see the worry on Mia's face, he guessed that she had anticipated that Paul's management skills had been tested and found wanting. But what would Rhys do? And where was Paul?

The last tree having been tamped into place, the lorry driver, his mate, and George came into the café for a well-earned cuppa. There was much discussion on the idea of a linear forest, and much hilarity at Rhys's suggestion of how long it would be before he could put up his aerial walkway.

The lorry departed and George drove the tractor into the shed and then walked sombrely over to the office with Rhys, neither wanting to start another conversation.

They were startled to find Paul already there, and the desk covered in paperwork.

Rhys sat down and George sat on the edge of a chair facing him.

'We all know this shouldn't have happened, from what I can understand there were a number of existing problems that led to today's events with a certain inevitability. And part of that was caused by the unforeseen absence of Joss to shore up the team while Anne was away. I appreciate that, but I need to understand why so many things appear to have been scheduled for the same day, without anybody realizing it. I thought you were supposed to have weekly meetings to plan and agree priorities. What happened? And I want a full explanation so just to reassure you, no one's job is on the line here. This is about avoiding anything like it happening again.

'Anyone?'

Paul looked dreadful, but he spoke up first.

'Look, Boss, I think it's mostly my fault, and I'm so sorry to let you and Anne down. I never realized the amount of paperwork involved in running a business, even taking it home I haven't caught up. I think it got to me so much I was more worried about getting forms wrong than managing everything that is going on here. What caused today was me forgetting to tell George about the change of tree delivery and not checking the diary about the school visit.'

George interrupted.

'I was the experienced manager here, and I didn't see how stressed Paul was with the paperwork, and I should have done. So, it's not fair for him to think he is the only one who cocked-up.'

'OK'. Rhys was beginning to see a theme, and a little light at last. 'First of all, apart from the paperwork is there anything else that is preventing you getting the work done and the planning back on track?'

'I think, once we get that new girl in the café, Mia might be able to give me a hand with the paperwork which will free me up to do everything else in the plan I agreed with Anne.' Paul was looking happier now he had spoken about his problem. 'It's not that I don't understand it, it's just the sheer quantity.'

'Another pair of hands anywhere in the team will help, as Paul said. And that new student is becoming more useful at the weekends, particularly now he can drive the tractor.' George sounded more confident. 'Apart from what we have both said, I think we can handle everything else with in our weekly meetings.'

Rhys was more reassured. 'I'm sure Anne used to

throw loads of that paper in the bin, but then she could take those decisions and I don't think she foresaw that you couldn't. I suggest the way forward is for Anne to draw up a simple list of criteria about what is important, what needs her decision, and what you can happily throw in the recycling. Then we will see if you still need help.'

29 A Serious Incident

'Hmmmm. I think that might have put the new business idea of Mia and Paul on hold for a bit. It's all very well swanning around with computer-generated garden layouts for people with deep pockets, but the more you work the greater the paper trail. And, no, it isn't possible to control it all on a mobile, especially if you have to employ people.' Anne was feeling sanguine about the need for Rhys's intervention after less than two weeks of Paul's stewardship. 'Did he really think he was going to lose his job?'

'Well, if he'd thought about it, I don't suppose he would have, but he panicked so anything seemed possible, I suppose. It will probably be a good thing for both him and the Park that it happened now. He will learn from it, and we shall have a better run business while you are away.'

'What?'

'Oh, you know what I mean, he'll be more careful, no one could ever run it like you do, my love.'

'Wait until I run that past again, it didn't sound like the ringing endorsement I'd hoped for. OK, so what about this new girl for the café, any good?'

'Best of the bunch, Mia said, and she has all the qualifications and is still employed at that little teashop in the town after a year, so I suppose that must say something. I took her on anyway, everybody is getting stretched without your brains and your dad's reliability.'

'No need to smarm it on, I've forgiven you. But

enthusiasm for the new girl, I am not hearing. What's her name, by the way?'

'Rowena. I'm more used to interviewing over twenty-year-olds, she is only seventeen and there is a big difference in maturity. I hope the Park Mothers won't try to get away with any scams. You remember that one who tried it on with Mia when she first started. 'I'm just leaving little Anthony in the café for a moment love, while I pick up his tea from the shops.' An hour later she turned up and you banned her for a fortnight.'

'Mia says she will keep a close eye on her and tell her which ones to look out for. And George or Paul will be around if there is any banning to be done.'

'I haven't had to ban anyone, except Arnie, since then. The word got round, and we didn't have any more trouble.' Anne sighed and looked at her little son. 'Don't you even think of cheeking a Park employee when you're older, or you'll end up digging flower beds for penance every weekend.'

It wasn't an adult who discovered that Rowena had a temper.

Arnie was growing up in many ways and, at twelve, was a big lad for his age. He eyed Rowena as being not a lot taller than him and not much different to some of the girls in his school, ready for a laugh and a bit of his cheek.

Mia had warned Rowena not to stand any nonsense from him, but he struck her as being very polite and just friendly. There was some banter between them on the couple of occasions he called in on his way home from school. But the next time he came in he had a couple of mates and was showing off, telling them she wanted to go out with him.

'In your dreams,' Rowena countered.

Then he put his hand under her skirt and started to

say 'You don't mean ...'

Which was as far as he got as she slapped his face so hard, he bit his tongue, and started crying. Rowena demonstrated a full range of vocabulary that left no doubt as to the impossible anatomical contortions he was expected to perform on himself and finished by announcing that her father was a sergeant in the Met Police and if he ever came near her again, she'd have him charged with assault.

The silence that followed was deepened as Paul turned off the lawnmower nearby. The three other Park Mothers stopped mid-gossip and Mia turned round from serving an elderly gentleman, who was the first to recover.

'That girl, was she in the Army? I haven't heard a swear like that since my Sergeant Major had his stick stolen.'

Mia and Paul arrived at the table together where Arnie had stopped crying, was rubbing his cheek, and trying to regain some dignity in front of his two pals, who were looking scared and trying to slink away.

Paul said, 'Mia, please take Rowena to the office and let her calm herself.'

Rowena cast a final, 'Dirty little pervert', and walked away grumbling to Mia.

Paul looked at Arnie and then asked his pals what had happened. They stuttered, but finally it came out that Arnie had tried to put his hand up Rowena's skirt. Paul wrote down their names and addresses and what they had said, all the while keeping an eye on Arnie.

'Right, young man, what have you got to say?'

'I'm sorry, but it was only a bit of fun. She didn't have to hit me like that. I might go to a solicitor; she could've knocked my teeth out.'

Paul considered saying that if he had done that to

Mia, he would have knocked his teeth out. But he was representing the Park, so he had better be careful.

'You do realise that what you did could be seen as a serious assault on one of our employees and it is not just her who might bring charges? In the meantime, I am banning you from the Park for six months, although Mr Banks may feel that is not enough when I report the matter to him.

'I'd suggest that you consider a full apology in the hope that both Rowena and Mr Banks will look at not taking any further action. Do you understand that, Arnie? We've had some run-ins over the years, but this is not kids' stuff and I hope your mother will understand that.

'Now, get off home.'

Paul made his way over to where George was repairing some fencing, explained what had happened and asked him if he could take over the café for a little while and give the few customers a free cup of tea, and sound out their reactions, in case there was any sympathy for Arnie. He needed Mia in the meeting with Rowena who might still be in a state and not feel safe with just a man there.

He needn't have worried, Rowena was still seething, but it was because a "little kid" had thought he was dealing with a "snotty nosed little classmate", whereas she was a woman.

Paul said he fully understood her anger, but she could have put herself in danger if he'd hit her back, he was a strong lad. If anything like that happened in the future, and they would all look out for anyone who might be suspicious, then the better way to handle it would be to come to any other member of staff and report it straight away and let them deal with the person. They all had walkie talkies and could be called from the café handset if required.

About her language, upset though she was, he advised her to consider the length of the tirade, although he was sure nothing like that would ever happen again.

In the meantime, was she considering taking it any further in relation to the assault charge?

Rowena was angrier with 'that kid thinking he could try it on,' than with the actual assault. She did confirm that her father was in the Met Police, but he'd left them about ten years ago and she hadn't heard from him since.

Mia took her home in Paul's car and returned with a smile that said, 'I knew she was a good choice; we won't have any trouble from awkward customers ever again.'

The old soldier said it was the most entertainment he had had in weeks, and he was coming every day now, just in case it all sparked off again.

Paul reported in detail to Rhys, who congratulated him on his handling of the situation and, if the attitude of the Park Mothers who were there was anything to go by, Arnie's mother wasn't going to be welcomed back by them very soon either.

30 Time Out

Joss was feeling so much better that Diane said she would allow him to go out for a walk, just round the block to see how he got on, and she would accompany him in case he needed an arm to hold onto.

They started out at a reasonable pace and did three sides of the block before Joss had to slow down and lean against a front garden wall for a moment. Diane was all for popping round the corner to get the car so she could drive him the rest of the way. She was also cursing herself for being too ready to believe he could get over pneumonia so quickly.

Joss would have none of it and insisted that holding her arm would be all the assistance he needed. After a few paces Joss straightened up and tucked her arm comfortably under his, smiled mischievously at her startled expression as she turned to face him and whispered, 'I just wanted to make it feel like we were out on a date, a couple of oldies, perhaps coming back from the cinema, just friends, chatting and being comfortable together. And it feels like that, you didn't pull away, so how about I ask you in for a cup of coffee?'

'Joseph, you are a fraud and as crafty as I remember. I bet this isn't the first time you have been out while I'd left you to go home to pick up clothes. The way you are walking now, admit it.'

'You have me there, although I did ask Samuel to come with me the first time in case I couldn't make it.'

'The first time?'

'Well, I had to be sure I could walk you home properly, so I've been walking in the garden and just up to the local shop to get you something special for tea tonight. And I looked up the internet for the cinema on Wednesday and thought we might try that, if I can work out how to order tickets online.'

'Only if we go Dutch.' But Diane was smiling as she nestled her arm closer to his jacket. She'd walked arm in arm with Alistair sometimes, but it hadn't felt like this. Somehow the warmth radiated by Joseph was not just physical, it surrounded her in a cloud of safety and caring that she hadn't known for many years. This man was weak in body as he recovered from the pneumonia, and vulnerable to the temptation of alcohol, which would never leave him, yet his closeness was a shield against the world that she had fought alone for so long. Perhaps anything was possible in their future.

Wednesday was forecast to be a sunny spring day, not overly warm but good enough to round off Rhys's paternity leave with a picnic. The motorcaravan came up trumps with plenty of room for the buggy, the dog, all the luggage for Oliver, the lad himself in car seat and the proud but now more experienced parents. Just a short trip to a favourite car park in the woods, there were few people about at this time of the year so Jem could run free as they pushed the buggy over tree roots and soft ground for the first time. It was so lovely to be out that they couldn't imagine why it had been such a fuss worrying about whether Oliver would take to being strapped in and moving in this large vehicle. Or concerned whether Jem would be jealous of the baby being in his moving kennel.

If anything, Oliver was more fascinated by his high viewpoint affording views from all around rather than just the tops of passing cars. Jem didn't seem to worry, although there was no indication that this, very smelly, human was likely to lay down in his favourite spot, clipped to a safety belt harness just behind the driver and passenger seats.

Anne squelched out of the van into a muddy puddle. 'I'll miss you when you go back to work next week.'

'I imagine you'd, double the workload for a start.'

'I'm being serious, Ree. I hadn't realized until now that we have both been so tied up with your work and me running the Park that "our" time had all but disappeared. Even having to share you with Oliver it's brought back all our old closeness, readily guessing the other's thoughts, talking about the future, even sharing worries about Dad, or doing some small repairs around the house. We mustn't lose that again, we need to make time for us every week, even if it is just having a film night when Oliver is asleep. And, I haven't read a fiction book in months, what with legal stuff that Mr Silk keeps sending me and environmental papers that Robin insists we should be considering, and that's without the pile of "first time parents" horror manuals.'

'I know,' Rhys was pushing the buggy with a determined look at the particularly muddy stretch of path that barred their way. 'Shall we go for it?'

'What?'

'The mud dash, you remember when we first came here with Jem, we held hands and made a run for it through the mud?'

'You'll tip the baby out of the buggy.'

'No. What you just said. We leave the buggy this side and run through the mud and back, but it won't be a race this time, just for the fun of it.'

They ran, with Jem streaking past them, and back, walking boots and trouser bottoms covered in mud splatters. The dog, covered from ears to tail, happily doing the crossing several times at full speed.

'We're bloody mad. What hope does this poor child have with daft parents like us? Come on, let's get back to the van, have a cup of tea and get cleaned up. Good job we bought our ordinary shoes with us. You can tie Jem up outside while I feed Oliver.'

The cool afternoon of late April prompted them to turn on the van's gas heating while they chatted, fed, and changed the baby, and enjoyed a cup of tea and a cake bought for the occasion.

'If only we knew where Dot was when she had the baby there might be a chance of looking for a birth certificate. I've tried a general search but can't find a Dorothy Flowers anywhere.' The excitement of their own baby had not diminished Anne's determination to continue the search.

Rhys was not sure they would ever find out, especially if the baby had been adopted straight away and registered in the new parent's name.

'I looked it up, and in the 1950s and 60s adoption was almost unregulated: it depended where you lived, how good the local councils were at trying to license adoption societies, and who you knew, I suspect.'

They were interrupted by Jem barking at them to remind everybody that he was missing the constant companionship he had enjoyed for the past few weeks. Rhys climbed out of the warm van and got to work with brush and comb on the mud-stained scruff that barked and skipped with excitement.

'Why don't we call in and see Mum and Dad on the way home? It'll be a nice surprise for them, and we can see how they are getting on.'

However, when they got there the house was in darkness. The new tenants had yet to move in, such were the complicated legal niceties for a first-time landlord, particularly coinciding with first-time parenthood.

'That's odd, no lights in the flat and Mum's car isn't here. I hope nothing has happened to Dad. Perhaps I should give Mum a ring.'

Before Anne could get to her phone a shadow waved at her through the passenger window.

'I thought that must be you, Anne. Nice wheels, by the way. Hi Rhys.' Samuel came closer as Anne's window slid silently open.

'Hallo Samuel, do you know where Mum and Dad are? I'm a bit worried there is no one in.'

'Oh, you have to make an appointment with those two now. Always out and about,' he exaggerated. 'Off to the pictures this afternoon, I think. All dressed up, Joss opening the car door for your mum to get in, like a couple of teenagers out on a date.'

'You're having me on, Samuel.' Anne looked for signs of a grin but found none.

'Honestly, always out in the garden pretending to look at the plants but laughing and then she "pretend" slaps his shoulder. Are you sure they're married? They don't act like any couple I know who've been married for so many years.'

Anne sat back and looked totally confused, Rhys, perhaps a more detached observer, just grinned and said one word, 'Breakfast?'

Now Samuel looked confused, but Anne sprung back to life. 'Don't start that again, Rhys Banks, not in front of the baby.' But she giggled as she said it.

Later, showered and getting ready for whatever sleep Oliver might allow them, Anne surprised Rhys with another idea.

'I know what I said this morning about wanting more "us" time but I keep thinking about the list you want me to give Paul about paperwork. I think I'd feel happier if I looked over anything he wasn't sure about, working out a definitive list would be tricky, and I could miss something important. He could drop the stuff over to me once or twice a week, it wouldn't take long to decide what he needs to do something about, and what I can bin. I'd be able to relax more if I didn't have that little niggle of his judgement. What do you think?'

'I started off thinking about the increased workload you'll have with me not being here. But I take your point and it'll mean you don't go back "cold" when you decide the time is right.'

On another subject, we ought to thank my parents for filling in at the café before we got the new girl. Could we lay on a little tea party soon, and invite your mum and dad to find out what stage this strange, already living together, courtship has reached?'

'Good thinking if a bit sneaky.'

31 Oliver Kieran Banks Visits the Park

Perhaps not so strangely, a similar conversation was taking place in the other Banks's household, where Bill and Jane were equally intrigued by the Joseph and Diane relationship. However, their reason for getting together was to tell the new parents what help they could offer in looking after Oliver when Anne took control of the Park at the end of Paul's six-month tenure. The plans they'd made together would have to change after Joseph's spell in hospital, of course. The fact that Rhys was returning to full- time work next week gave them the excuse to contact him and suggest a meeting.

Meanwhile, on their return from the cinema and being told of Anne's reaction to Samuel's account of their "date", Diane felt obliged to explain to her daughter what the situation was. If only she could get it clear in her own mind.

Rhys was fastest off the mark and was surprised at the enthusiastic response from his parents, which he was just conveying to Anne, when her phone rang and Diane proposed to visit them, 'to talk about things, as we missed you the other evening.'

On top of the parents known diary no-no's, Wednesday morning Bowling club – Jane, Thursday evening Photographic society – Bill, Thursday morning Doctor's appointment – Joss, and Monday afternoon U3A – Diane, Rhys had laid down that it had to be at the latest the coming Saturday, as he'd be preparing for work on Sunday and after that he had no idea when he'd have a free day.

In the meantime, there was another important engagement, Oliver's first visit to the Park. Rhys had checked the weather forecast and Friday looked dry so he arranged it with George and Paul but swore them to secrecy, knowing that every Park Mother would descend on the Park once word got out, and he and Anne wanted to have some time with the staff first.

Of course, it didn't happen that way. Somehow, although separately, – Dennis, ex-ice cream man, as well as Doreen Cattermole and husband, Chief Planning Officer, Arnold, chose that very day to catch up with the Park's green developments.

Mr Silk and Ethel, wife and secretary, and sometime wild flamenco dancer, were "just passing" and thought they would pop in and see what legal pitfalls had developed since their last visit, at the wedding. The public charger points for visitors' cars had him scribbling a note to check their Public Liability insurance.

Even Gerry, their accountant, was there to discuss a minor financial matter with Paul.

Which would have constituted a full afternoon for young Oliver, without every green space being full of well wrapped picnickers being assembled by a visibly ebullient Councillor Broome and local reporter, Martin, accompanied by a harassed looking photographer.

Their first hint of the reception awaiting them was as they approached the road leading to the Park entrance, and Mark, the local policeman, stepped out to hold up the traffic coming the other way, and waved them in.

Space had been marked out for them in the car park otherwise they would never have got in. Rhys considered reversing out anyway, until he saw the crowds clapping and phones flashing.

'Remember your Young Ladies Academy training,

Anne. Knees together as you exit the seat, big smile and don't bend over in that dress to get Oliver out, I'll do that.'

'Hell's Bells, Ree. I thought you told them to keep it a secret. And I do know how to get out of a car, thank you. How do you think I got on in Mum's ''bum on the tarmac'' sports car?'

'That was one of the highlights of my day every time you borrowed the car. Right. We're on, just keep an eye on that photographer.'

Fortunately, George's wife had guessed what might happen and given him strict instructions not to let people crowd around and frighten the baby. The Park staff had organized people as they arrived and directed them to places where the couple could come and talk to them in small groups.

All that went out the window as the car arrived, and now every member of staff, including the new girl was engaged in getting the crowd back to their designated spots. It had to be said that Rowena was having no trouble with her group.

Apart from Anne being hugged by the almost sober Councillor, and a peck on the cheek by Gerry, the most photographed event was Doreen Cattermole throwing her arms round a startled Rhys and hugging him, for perhaps a few seconds longer than the wife of a senior Council Officer should have.

An hour and a half later, Anne declared that Oliver was getting tired and needed a feed so they would have to say goodbye. They escaped with a big bag filled with teddy bears, sun hats, even some knitted clothes, and over fifty cards from small to a two-foot-tall greeting from the football teams, signed by every player.

Spring was showing the changes in the Park for the first time. All the trees in the lateral mini forest were planted and coming into leaf. It would be a few years before an aerial walkway could be tried, but a miniature rope ladder had been tied to the tops and squirrels were already using it before leaping off to forage lower down in the branches.

The hedges now covered the metal fencing all around the Park and new colonies of birds, insects and small mammals were establishing themselves.

It was too early for the wildflower plots to show their colour, but other new ideas, like the various composting methods, worm farms and insect hotels were beginning to feature in the school tours led by Robin and the new part-time worker, Asaf.

Asaf had been employed when it became clear that Joss would not be returning to the heavy workload anytime soon. With a degree in horticulture and a passion for the environment he was a natural ally of Robin, but Paul had taken him on because he was young, fit and needed a year of practical work to put on his CV. His initial contract was for six months as Joss might return, or Anne might not want to continue the arrangement when she took over from Paul.

However, between them, Robin and Asaf made a formidable team pushing the self-sufficiency agenda of the Park, with ideas for using wind power and heat pumps.

'Way beyond my pay grade,' Paul told them, 'That is serious capital expenditure that I can tell you the Park hasn't got. It'll mean borrowing, so you'd better get some solid income or cost reduction figures down the line if you want Anne to even consider it.'

They did have a rather surprising ally in George. He'd been reading extensively about climate change and ways to combat it and could see the way the Park was able to demonstrate small steps in practical terms but also have a much larger influence in educating not only the schoolchildren but the whole community who used the Park. From heating the showers in the football and tennis changing rooms to the replacement of all lighting with LED's, to a tractor sharing arrangement with the farm next door, George knew every part of the routine and equipment inside out. He proposed that every change they made should be signposted with the reasons why, even down to the saving of fossil fuel by turning the lake fountain pump off at night.

A clash between the family-centred Park and the environmental-centred Park looked like being Anne's big decision area when she returned to take over the reins again.

32 Grandparents

The family get together, with three different agendas, started with much passing around of a somewhat startled Oliver, sometimes laughing, sometimes lip quivering on the verge of tears. Eventually, dropping off to sleep and being put in his cot, baby alarm switched on, the adults sat down to talk.

Rhys started off by thanking his mum and dad for helping at the café in the emergency between Anne going into hospital and the new assistant starting. Jane was quick to jump in and say not only had they enjoyed it but, obviously they hadn't been as entertaining to the customers as the new girl in her first week.

'You've heard,' groaned Rhys, 'How on earth did you find out?'

'We were talking to Diane and Joseph, and Joseph had been talking to, well, somebody at the Park.'

Anne's antenna, already quivering after the mysterious meeting of the parents, vibrated into speech. 'What's going on? You four are hiding something, tea parties and phone calls, and now you're all looking guilty as hell. Mum, what have you been hatching?'

'Calm down, Anne, you'll upset the baby's milk.' Diane had a definite twinkle in her eye. 'Yes, we've been getting together, and very pleasant it's been. Bill and Jane have been so understanding of the weird situation your father and I find ourselves in. But we'll come to that later. I think Jane should explain.'

Jane's amusement was infectious. 'First of all, I

should say that this has nothing to do with any recent management hiccoughs, yes we heard about those as well. We started talking about this some time ago and it's really just to give you both some options, if you're happy with the ideas, both in the short term and possibly a bit longer.'

She paused.

'Come on, Mother, don't stop now, you've got our full attention, don't tease.' Rhys smiled and pointedly drummed his fingers on the arm of his chair.

'Well, it's quite simple, the four of us have agreed that we'll be available to look after Oliver if Anne wants to take on some work at the Park, before the six months are up of Paul being in day-to-day charge. We know that you're keen to look at the changes to an ecology centre idea, something that only you can do, and this would give you time to sit down and plan for the future while Paul is still in charge.

Raising her hand before anyone could jump in, she continued.

'The difficulty we had to overcome was how to do it without moving carloads of baby things around the different houses. There really is only one solution, we will look after Oliver here. That way he has all his familiar things around him, the dog can go in and out, and might even get a walk, or two, and we can get some washing done and out on the line on good days. It also allows for all our other activities to continue if we get the days sorted. I think that's about it.'

Before Anne or Rhys could recover, Diane chimed in to explain how Joseph's spell in hospital had affected the plan.

'The other night you came round, and we'd gone to the pictures and if you were confused about our relationship believe me, so were we. Despite living in the flat together it took that visit to see a film to get us both feeling the same way. We want to try and make a go of it second time around. Or, to answer you Rhys, you cheeky so and so, we now have breakfast together.

'What this means for looking after Oliver is, I'll be staying at the flat, but keeping my other place on, in case it doesn't work out, we've been honest about that. So, we can be easily available as a team with Bill and Jane.'

Anne launched herself at her mum and dad, tearful and hugging and setting them all off, handkerchiefs all round.

Jane recovered first and said, 'I'll just go and put the kettle on.' But didn't get there before getting a big hug from her son.

Bill jumped in to complete the suggestion, although he wasn't sure anyone was listening.

'What we've also talked about is possibly continuing the arrangement after Anne goes back to managing the Park, possibly up to or beyond Oliver going to nursery. So, you see we've thought this through, but obviously it's up to you two whether you think it is a good idea.'

Later, with Anne still sitting on the floor in front of her parents and holding a hand of each, they all calmed down and discussed the details of how it might work.

33 A Clue at Last?

The next months passed very quickly with Oliver gaining a personality, Anne gaining time to be a mother, a wife, a daughter, and a business planner. And Rhys? He gained the serenity of a family to balance the responsibilities his high-pressure job demanded.

The six months of Paul running the Park were nearly up, and Anne was getting nervous about what his plans would be now he'd experienced the sharp end of taking decisions on a daily basis. Admittedly, he wasn't risking his own finances, and the Park was now an established, if precarious, business, but the fact was he'd made a few mistakes, and learned from them. Was he ready to take that leap into running his own garden planning enterprise? Did he have the financial backing or savings to see him through the start-up phase? More importantly, how were they going to manage at the Park without him?

Paul's great skill was in planning displays, picking the right plants to make sure the Park was a riot of colour and shape throughout the seasons. In that respect his skills would be less needed as the Park transitioned to more eco displays. But his importance in such a small team outweighed his skill. He, Robin, and George had worked together for years before Rhys had inherited the Park. Their commitment to Dot's dream of a community within the Park had been a major factor in persuading Rhys to accept the challenge that Dot left him. Taking Paul out of the equation, and with George due to retire in a year or two, plus the likelihood that her dad wouldn't be returning to his job for some time, if ever, Anne was under pressure to replace them. But also, the opportunity to re-model the Park with people enthusiastic and knowledgeable about her eco vision. But it all depended on Paul.

The six months was up, and Paul confessed to Mia he had mixed feelings on starting a business. He'd learned a lot about legal matters, finance, organisation, and his own strengths and weaknesses. His major concern was having the money to pay the mortgage on his flat until he established regular clients.

With Mia working alongside him, their hopes of starting their own business were encouraged by every decision they got right and dampened by wrong paths. The latter had become fewer as the months passed but Mia only had her income from working in the café, as she was still studying, not nearly enough for them to live on. Gradually they had worked up a proposal for Anne.

Their Hampstead project had proved profitable in both financial and reputation referrals. They couldn't survive on the work they had, and they couldn't take on any more work because of the time Paul was working at the Park. But, if Anne would agree, Paul would work three days a week for the next six months at the Park and the rest of the time he'd build his small workforce and go after more contracts. After six months he'd go full time in his own business, and Mia might join him. That gave Anne certainty until next spring by which time she'd be able to employ someone to take the Park into the ecology direction she wanted.

Rhys and Anne agreed that this was a fair plan, after all, Dot had "stolen" Paul from the Council parks

Department because he was an excellent plantsman and visionary designer. But the Park was changing, and the flower beds were going to be fewer, so Robin and George could handle the limited design work. Using more of the space for ecology projects, that needed less labour and opened the possibility of employing someone to market the Park. They would need someone who was adept with taking over the website that Paul had organized, plus creating content for all the other marketing the internet offered.

The babysitting arrangements with the parents had worked well, barring a dispute when Rhys and Anne insisted that their parents should be paid, complicated by Diane claiming that she was effectively a tenant and should be paying them rent.

They compromised on everybody being taken for a slap-up meal and a show in the West End every so often. And Diane being reimbursed exactly the rent she wanted to pay, for her expenses in having to travel backwards and forwards to her old flat while looking after Joseph. Honour satisfied all round.

'There's nothing wrong.' Anne gripped her pencil tighter, Mum didn't usually phone when they were looking after Oliver.

'If there's nothing wrong, why are you phoning me? What's wrong?'

'Nothing is wrong, Oliver and your dad are playing in the garden and I'm reading a book. Or, at least, I thought I was. I've been going through Dot's book collection trying to find anything worth reading. Some of it's quite high-brow, some is unreadable by anyone without a Masters in the subject.'

'This I know, Mum, so why have you phoned me?'

'I'm coming to that. I brought a few books with me

from one of the higher shelves, got your dad to hold the little stepladder while I picked them.'

'And?'

'Well, one of them isn't a book. It looks like a book, but it opens as a box with loads of cuttings and little notes, I assume written by Dot.'

'What are all the cuttings about, Mum?' Anne's voice was tinged with excitement.

'Oh, no help to you, I'm afraid. They are all about Jane, her sister, growing up and at school. She must have been sent them by their mother because Dot was in London, living her own busy life. To keep her up to date, that was nice of her, wasn't it? I just thought you would like to know; in case you want to look for any more books that are really boxes.'

Anne breathed out. Was this why they couldn't find anything, because Dot had hidden it in plain sight? Somewhere in that bookcase might be the answer she so desperately wanted to find.

'You know Rhys is at some conference until tomorrow? When I come home can I sort out Oliver and then come round with him and have a look in the bookcase?'

'I'd rather you waited until Rhys was here to hold the ladder steady, your dad gets a bit wobbly after a while, I had to get down.'

'OK, tomorrow then, I'm working at home and Ree should be home mid-afternoon. We'll have a meal and come round about seven, would that be alright?'

That night, when Rhys phoned, she couldn't keep the excitement out of her voice. 'I know it's there Ree, somewhere she has another hidden book, or more and there will be a clue, something that will take us on the next step.'

There were two more fake books, but they were empty save for a business card for Mr Silk. Anne was distraught.

'That's what must be in the box Mr Silk has in his office, the contents of these two boxes. We're never going to find her, Ree. Dot has set up a circular lock, we can't find the clue to get Mr Silk to open the box because the only clue is in that box.'

'Look, love, did it ever occur to you that Dot doesn't want her daughter found by anyone? Unless the daughter has part of the clue and either doesn't know it or isn't interested in finding out who her mother was.'

'Dot loved her daughter.' Joss had been quiet up till then but spoke with certainty.

'Dad, what do you mean, she loved her daughter? Did she say something, have you remembered something?'

'No, she never said anything, I would have told you. But it was the way she looked at a little girl in the Park sometimes, not always the same one. Her face would soften, and she wouldn't hear what you said for a moment or two. I thought it was just that she liked kids, which she did. She didn't have the faintest idea about bringing them up, even though she used to lecture the Park Mothers. But there were those odd times. It's no help as I can't remember who they were or what they looked like; my memory was a bit fragile in those days. But I know she must have loved her daughter.'

Anne couldn't hide her emotions as she walked over to his chair and hugged him.

'That tells me a lot. It says she didn't give up her child easily. That the little girl was always there in her mind. I wonder if the girl in the Park reminded her of the last time she saw her daughter, or it was a significant age when something changed?'

'I expect Jane would like the other box.' Diane reminded them. 'Here, Rhys, better give it to her.'

'Thanks, I think we'd better get Oliver home now, and Anne looks as though a hot chocolate, and an early night would do her good. I've a breakfast meeting in the office tomorrow, good job youngsters started sleeping through the night, we could all do with a good night's sleep.'

34 A Shocking Offer

Rhys was contemplating an invitation from his boss for a meeting in Amsterdam to look at a possible acquisition of a Dutch company. If it went ahead the sales side would be handled from the UK, in other words, Rhys.

He took a call on his private mobile from Gerry, the accountant for the Park.

'Need to see you, and Anne, in my office tomorrow at ten thirty. Don't tell me you can't make it, postpone everything, throw a sickie; just get here.'

'Hold on, Gerry, I might be going to Amsterdam. What's it all about?'

'Amsterdam, lovely city but it will still be there the day after tomorrow, and I cannot tell you what it is about, sorry, really can't. Just get here.'

Office meetings with Gerry generally meant serious or bad news, this sounded very serious or very bad. Anne could get away as it was her mum's turn to babysit while Anne worked at the Park. Rhys told his boss he needed to do some work on the Dutch idea before committing any resources to it, and twenty-four hours wouldn't affect any of the technical agreements the lawyers were working on.

Gerry met them in reception assured them it wasn't bad news, and took them through to the biggest meeting room, where three men in suits stood to greet them.

Having introduced the men by name, Gerry mentioned the company they worked for, which meant nothing to either Anne or Rhys.

'You probably won't have heard of us,' said the obvious leader of the group. 'We tend to be publicity shy in our business.'

Anne thought "Mafia", but then remembered Gerry's reassurance.

'We work for some of the biggest names in the retail food industry, locating places with strong long-term potential and Chip Notting has been assessed as a future hub for development. There are serious talks going on with the local Council, developers, and commercial interests and so we must ask that whatever we tell you remains confidential.

'Obviously, with major development there will be a need for good quality housing and infrastructure, schools, doctors' surgeries and the like. And shops, supermarkets in fact.

'At this very early stage, we are probably looking at a time frame of fifteen to twenty years for the complete project. However, our clients, who I cannot name, are interested in purchasing sufficient land for their element of the project on the assumption that it will go ahead.

'On that basis we have surveyed likely sites and your Park has the quantity of land that would suit a large supermarket with petrol station and encompass the necessary car parking area. We are aware of the covenant, which runs out in 2026 we believe, but our Principals have authorized us to open negotiations with you on purchasing the site now with a view to you running the business until 2026 before vacating the site.

'We should point out that this is a very speculative investment by our clients, which means that if you do not accept the offer at this stage, and the whole project is abandoned, there will be no future offers. And we are actively looking at other areas in the town.

'We have discussed this with your accountant only to

the point where we could set up this meeting.'

Rhys interrupted him, 'It isn't a business, it's a community, I have no intention of selling.'

'Totally agree,' said Anne.

'Yes, your accountant did say that you may be initially very opposed to selling, but please hear me out. Our clients are willing to start negotiations at five million pounds for all the land, vacated by 2026. Just think what that could mean for not only you, but your son and any subsequent children.'

Rhys and Anne stared at one another in total disbelief. Rhys recovered first.

'Gerry, is this for real?'

'I'm afraid so, I know what that Park means to you – what it meant to your Aunt Dot. But this is a business proposal pure and simple and, as your accountant I must advise you to take it seriously. No need for decisions today, nobody expects you to take in the full implications at once, but please don't reject it out of hand. Remember, I'm on your side so anything you want to discuss you know you can call me anytime. But do you have any immediate questions for these gentlemen? Otherwise, I think we can diary another meeting in a fortnight's time for you to give a considered reaction. I would also suggest you contact Mr Silk for his legal opinion on the offer. I feel sure he will have many good reasons why five million can only be considered the starting point for negotiations.'

After the three men in suits had left, the two remaining men in suits and one woman in a dress sat around a coffee table in Jerry's office in stunned silence.

'Are you still going to Amsterdam, or would it be better to take the rest of the week off?' Gerry tried to start the conversation on a lighter note.

'Five million pounds.' Anne was still trying to process the enormous amount that the Park was worth to a supermarket.

'And some. If they offered that, it's probably worth seven or eight.' Rhys was putting his business brain in gear.

'But Ree, we couldn't sell out Dot's dream, our dream, we bought into it on that first visit, when you proposed, remember?'

'How could I forget. But think what it would mean for all the family, to be financially independent.'

'And do what? Sit on our backsides in the sun for the next forty years? Overindulge the kids so they care for nothing but money? My mum and dad don't need much, although Mum needs to get rid of that skateboard she calls a car before it falls apart altogether. But money wouldn't make them happier than they are now. Your mum and dad seem content, I suppose they might take more holidays, but I can't see it changing their lives that much.

'And, honestly Ree, would we give up working, perhaps not for somebody else, just ourselves? But I'm doing that now, and so are you, in a way.'

'Hey you two, I'm here. Gerry, remember? I asked you about Amsterdam because someone has to be the adult here. Decide what you are doing in your present life, you have the rest of the day, and then talk about this tonight. Call me anytime and let's meet in the pub, I'm your friend as well as your accountant.'

'Gerry, if you weren't already married and if I wasn't already married, I'm sure we could make heavenly music together. In the meantime, you get my best hug for knowing that this isn't a business decision for us, it's much more important.' Anne threw in a kiss on the cheek, and the shocked secretary next to the glass-walled office hit a string of kkkkkkkkkkkk's on her screen.

Rhys did some work on the Dutch proposal and then

told his boss that the business could integrate with the UK for many purposes, but sales was not among them. Apart from the language the market was set up differently and the structure was not similar enough for him to run it, far better to promote from within or buy in a Sales Director from a rival company.

Anne went back to the Park and looked at it with fresh eyes, community, fresh air, and Eco Park. If they sold up would anyone replace those assets to the town?

Surely, if the town was going to grow it would need those things more? Shouldn't open spaces be on the list of infrastructure?

Obviously, she needed an expert and who better than the Head of Planning, Mr Cattermole, after all he was very helpful over the electric car charging. The switchboard at the Council was aware that all calls from the Park had to go straight to Mr Cattermole ever since the battles with Dot had kept the Council Officers entertained for years.

Anne exchanged pleasantries and then asked a hypothetical question about a town that might be expanding and the need for public park provision at the planning stage.

There was a very long pause.

'Mr Cattermole ... Arnold, are you there?'

'Sorry, Mrs. Banks, hypothetical questions are always difficult. Can I ask, was there a particular reason for this "hypothetical" question?'

'Well, you know, we are always thinking ahead at the Park, look at our ecology projects.'

'I see, well there is no planning law that gives set figures, so it is up to each Council to interpret the regulations to fit their goals. Sorry, not much help I'm afraid. However, should an area be designated green belt, or agricultural land, then a lot more hurdles must be overcome before building is allowed. Perhaps you and Mr

Banks would like to make an appointment to review the Park's designation? With your latest activities perhaps a new classification might be more appropriate.'

'Thank you, Mr Cattermole, useful advice as always, I will tell my husband what you sugg— said.'

That night, after Oliver had been played with, and listened to a goodnight story, which he was too young to understand but made him go to sleep quicker, Anne and Rhys sat down for a serious talk about what they wanted in their life.

'There are three possibilities as I see it, we sell, we don't sell, or we get compulsorily purchased by the Council to make room for their masterplan.' Rhys looked gloomy.

'I think there may be a fourth option.' And Anne relayed her conversation with Arnold Cattermole.

35 Anne Closes the Gates

Rhys, having divested himself of any involvement in the Dutch takeover, took a week's leave and set Mr Silk the task of looking at what options the Council might have if the Park turned the enormous offer down. The solicitor's amazement at such a course of action was soon tempered when Rhys pointed out that, while the sale might be worth a one-off chunk of money to him, that would be the end of their business together, whereas keeping the Park could result in regular business for years to come.

While waiting for the legal information, prior to meeting the Council, Rhys asked Gerry to investigate the financial implications of turning the Park into a trust.

'So, you are going to turn this offer down, is that what you are telling me?' Gerry was surprised at the way Rhys and Anne had made such a swift decision without consulting him.

'Not necessarily, Gerry. But we do want to have all our options thoroughly examined. If the Council can compulsorily purchase the Park from me, as the owner, would a trust stop them? Obviously, if you can think of any other financial defences, please investigate those as well, and we will meet with both yourself and Mr Silk on Friday, which will give us another week to make decisions and talk to the Council.'

Anne assessed her options from the effect the Park closure could have on the staff, the Park users, and the wider community. As opposed to the effect all that money would have on her family.

George would have retired, Paul would have left, Asaf would have completed his year's practical experience, which just left Robin, who they could afford to pay a handsome lump sum. Plus, any other staff they would have taken on with short-term contracts up to 2026.

The Park users included the four football teams, the tennis club, the model yacht group, the Majorettes, and the Chip Notting Town Band. Not forgetting the Park Mothers, a group with connections all over the town. But probably the biggest losers would be the local schools, who used the educational facilities and expertise of the staff so extensively throughout the year.

Where would they all go? Not to the Council's own parks which were either well used already or discouraged such involvement in favour of sedate flower displays.

Then there was the wider community, the families who turned up occasionally for a day out and flocked to the Park in hot weather to have picnics under the trees while the younger ones played safely on the climbing frames and swung on ropes over sandy drop zones. Most of them walked to the Park, they would need a car or bus to get to other parks.

Out would go the plans to develop the Ecology Park idea, the developers would rip out all the newly planted trees, the worm and beetle homes, probably drain the lake used so extensively for pond dipping.

Anne stood in her office overlooking the Park, much as Dot would have done every day, and had to turn away so that people couldn't see the tears.

And what would £5, £6, or even £7 million do for her family? She and Rhys would never have to work again for anyone else. They could travel the world or look around to start another business, no idea what. Their children wouldn't want for anything, except perhaps to understand the value of something, not just its price.

They could give money to good causes, make a difference. But isn't that what they were doing now?

Anne's sadness turned to anger. How dare they think they could trample all over the community lovingly built by Dot and nurtured under their watch, just to build another brick edifice and tarmacked carpark to enhance a multi-million-pound balance sheet owned by people who had never heard of Chip Notting? No doubt they would have rafts of highly paid lawyers to batter the Council to grant planning permission for the whole scheme, and compulsory purchase any landowner who failed to sell.

Anne marched out of the office, down the stairs and amazed George by giving him a hug as she made her way to the gates. Robin was nearby, tidying up some leaves.

'Robin,' Anne called, 'it's about time these gates shone in their full glory again. Could you get me an estimate for a good painter to renew the black paint and the gold leaf marking the name, Ladywood Park?

'"Here we will plant our flag." Not sure where that is from but it's appropriate.'

36 Let Battle Commence

That night Rhys and Anne held a council of war. With Oliver asleep after his nightly story, and the dog walked, they settled down to assess their different approaches.

'Of course, if we turn down their offer, and then their "improved" offer, they might just give up and go to another site, if that option wasn't just bluff. But we must be prepared for a fight, possibly with the Council, and the Chief Planning Officer, Mr Cattermole, will have to do whatever the Councillors decide, whatever his private feelings might be.'

Anne agreed. 'I'm sure he doesn't want to see the Park go, if we get a change of status in quickly, we might strengthen his hand a bit. And we might get some support from Councillor Broome and one or two others who can see the difference we make to the community.

'But, at the end of the day, if we are holding up the whole Chip Notting development, I think the Council will vote against us. We need to start a campaign with the Park users to see off this development, timed to coincide with the local elections.'

Rhys was not so sure that they could start anything until the whole thing became public. 'Which could take months, if not years for plans and public consultations to go through. We don't want to peak too early.'

But Anne was on a roll. 'I've an idea for getting people and groups on board before they even know about the proposals. Let's name all our new trees and get schools and groups to sponsor their own choice, maybe a fiver a year, or something. Then they can measure their growth, add fertiliser, dance round it, I don't know, but take ownership of that little piece of the Park.'

Anne was excitedly tramping up and down the carpet while Rhys sat on the sofa feeling he was at Wimbledon.

'We could run a competition to see whose tree had grown the most in a year, perhaps hang a star on the winner each year.' Pausing for breath, but only for a moment. 'And, and, and,' her brain finally caught up with her mouth, 'I bet there are national or even international competitions, or recognition for organisations doing the most to promote ecology awareness in their area. That would make the Council reluctant to vote to destroy the Park, if we had international support.'

At last Rhys got a word in edgeways. 'Listen, my lovely Boudicca, I'm not sure you should be at the meeting with the Suits next week, not if you turn up in a chariot with scythes on the wheels, I think that would be classified as intimidation on a grand scale. My, I'd forgotten how beautiful you are in defence of your brood. I agree with every idea you've had, but I trump it with one of my own. How about an early night?'

The meeting with Mr Cattermole was a delicate balancing act of him explaining the options for having the land owned by the Park reclassified, without giving any hint of why it might be advantageous. To make sure that none of his careful descriptions could be misinterpreted later, he had a colleague sit in taking minutes, which Rhys could appreciate but had Anne fuming when they got outside.

'I was virtually silenced because every time I wanted to ask something, I realised it would give away our knowledge of the project, and then Mr Cattermole would have had to stop the meeting in case he could be accused of giving us advice to oppose a Council plan.'

'I know, but he did his best and now we can discuss the options with Mr Silk and Gerry. The foundations of our case are beginning to build upon your more "direct action" ideas. Which reminds me, why are we spending significant amounts of money on repainting the gates, which wasn't in the repair budget?'

'We are planting our flag, thus far and no further. The gates are where we will defend the Park when we need to. I don't mean physically, but with crowds of supporters and photo ops, all in front of the magnificent gates your grandfather designed?

'I've also moved ahead with the tree naming, as well. Those saplings are going to be reaching for the stars ...'

''So, we are going to call them Elvis and ...' Rhys interrupted.

'No! Don't you start, Dad said the same when I mentioned it to him.'

'You didn't tell him why you were doing it, did you?'

'Of course not. Now, back to the stars, there are plenty to choose from and I've already alerted Robin to the idea so that he can contact the schools to choose their own, and for £20, not a fiver, they could have their own nameplate carved by Robin, incorporating the school's name. Paul is contacting the sports clubs and George will be talking to the other groups, I think there are just enough trees to go round.'

Rhys looked at Anne, all fired up, and said quietly. 'Just tell me you've thought seriously about just taking the money and leaving. We really haven't sat down and discussed it since that first night. I know you're spoiling for a fight, and I know how much the Park means to both of us, but I also need to know that you've considered the alternative and what that money might mean for our family, a family that might be much bigger than it is today if our plans work out.'

Anne stopped walking and swung round to look at Rhys, the startled look on her face turning to a serious stare, the interrogation going deeper into his heart than at any time since the night they met. And then she smiled, 'You know I have, and I know you have, and it doesn't change a thing, does it? Dot left us something more precious than £5 million pounds, she left us as custodians of five million smiles, five million laughs and five million hopes. Over the years already gone, and in years to come, we will redeem those, with interest.

'Now come on, let battle commence!'

37 Winners and Losers

The meeting with their accountant and solicitor started with an analysis of the offer and what it might mean for the Banks family. Both Mr Silk and Gerry ended with professional recommendations that Rhys should accept the offer, after it had been upgraded by negotiation.

Rhys and Anne listened intently, made some notes, and then formally rejected both recommendations.

'OK, 'said Gerry, 'I think you are both mad, but then I thought that the night you presented me with a Harrods bag full of your aunt's accounts and said you wanted to take on an almost bankrupt Park, somewhere in Essex. What do you think, Mr Silk?'

'After years of working with Dot, where financial and legal realities took second place to her heart and gut instinct, I'm really not surprised at your decision. I would caution though, that however hard I work to achieve your goal of seeing off this offer, the longer it goes on the more the legal fees will mount as I have to bring in specialist associates. Let's see if we can prevent this going any further as soon as possible.'

The meeting with the representatives of the supermarket was intense, almost brutal, as the changed status of the Park, plus the intention to fight any kind of compulsory purchase with support from the community, local politicians at elections, and through the courts, were outlined. Increased offers were rebutted as irrelevant, amazement on the faces of the Suits treated as proof that they represented those who thought they knew the price but didn't understand the value of community.

When a second meeting, with yet more money on the table, produced the same response, the negotiations were suspended by the supermarket.

Within a month word came to Rhys, through a convoluted grapevine, which may, or may not, have had its roots in the Council, that another site had been judged to be more amenable to financial persuasion.

There was a big celebration called for all the users of the Park, although nobody quite knew why, at which the newly painted gates were unveiled and a toast to Dot eloquently made by Rhys, while Anne danced with many of the guests to music supplied by a friend of Paul's, who just happened to be a DJ.

38 Revelation!

To the delight of both parents and grandparents, six-month-old Oliver discovered that he could crawl. The downside was that they all had to be on their guard every minute he was awake. The sound of water splashing in the dog's bowl was cut short as Anne retrieved it and put it in the sink, only to turn round and realise, to her horror, that the empty but dirty dog food bowl was the next attraction for her escapee. More awkward was what to do with the dog as he was old and didn't mind Oliver laying his head on his stomach when he was stretched out, but he did object to his hair being used as a rope ladder as the young human tried to climb over him. Jem didn't bite, but he barked, loudly. Oliver slid off crying and Anne realized that she'd have to keep them apart until Oliver understood that they could be friends, but not cuddle friends.

Child gates were installed, and peace was restored, until Oliver discovered he could throw soft toys over the gate and Jem would always run and bring them back to him, pushing them through the bars and barking for more. Shouting and barking became a well-established part of the day whoever was looking after the two "kids".

What with work and playing with Oliver it was fully two weeks before Rhys remembered he hadn't given his mum the box of memories that Diane had found in the bookcase. It was in the car, and he was staying in yet another soulless hotel room, this one in Peterborough, after a full day with the Midlands sales team. He had given his excuse of urgent paperwork and left the National Sales Manager to organize any entertainment after the evening meal. It was another hour before he was due to phone Anne, and the charts he had taken out of his bag were beginning to merge before his tired eyes.

A breath of fresh air, if only to the car park, and bring in the box and find out what his mum had been up to as a youngster, he was looking forward to teasing her.

But it turned out that extracts of school reports, short notes from their mother to Dot saying how Jane was getting on, and a newspaper cutting mentioning Jane having won a prize for swimming, didn't add up to much teasing material. There were also some scraps of paper underneath in what Rhys recognised as Dot's handwriting detailing more of Jane's achievements, A* for an essay, disappointing C+ in maths test, scored goal in inter-school girls' football. Each stark fact with date was accompanied by a comment which made Rhys grin or feel sad for his mum. Finally, there was a single photo, obviously taken when Jane started at her secondary school, smiling, and waving at the camera. He had seen it before in one of the old photo albums, the tall young woman beside her he now realised must be Dot, they were very alike when they smiled, but Dot had dark hair and Jane was blonde, and still was.

But something was niggling him. He suddenly realised that the comments were all made by Dot, for Dot. There was no indication that she ever intended to express those views directly to Jane, or why had she needed to write them down?

He looked at all the comments again, 'Not what I would have done', 'I don't know why you're not better at maths, it was my favourite subject', 'You're too quiet, I was never a mouse at school, you didn't get that from me', and 'I love you so much, but you are going to have to stand up to Mother, I can't be there for you.' And others in the same vein.

He turned the photo over and stared at Dot's comment. 'So proud of you, my darling daughter, how I wish I could hug you as only a mother can.'

He lay back on the bed and whispered, 'My God! My Bloody God. Hell, hell, hell. Surely not? How could it be? It couldn't happen. Or could it? What the hell am I going to do now?'

What he did was ring room service for a large Americano, with an extra shot. He sat unmoving until it came, drank it scalding hot and then settled down to re-read every bit of paper in the box. After which he drank a cup of the hotel supplied Nescafé and phoned Anne.

'Is Oliver in bed?'

'Yes, and good evening to you, and also, yes, I've had a productive day, the Park has not burned down, our creditors are being kept at bay by the ginormous guard dog, Jem. So, all is well in the Banks household. Why are you so abrupt? Has something happened?'

Now, Anne was beginning to sound uneasy.

'If it happened, it happened fifty odd years ago. This is not bad news, but it is, I think shocking news so I should sit down or get yourself a cup of coffee if you want.'

'Ree, stop waffling, I don't need to sit down or get a coffee, what I want is for you to tell me what is happening. I'm really worried now.'

'As I said, there is nothing bad in this but ...'

'Ree, I'm at screaming point, just tell me.'

'OK. You know that box of papers that your mum found, and gave to me to give to my mum? Well, I forgot about them until this evening and thought I'd see what she got up to, to tease her, but I've read them, and then re-read all the comments Dot made, with a strong coffee in between to make sure I wasn't imagining things. And there is a photograph with Dot's writing. Anne, I don't think Mum is Dot's sister, I think she is Dot's daughter.'

There was a silence for a second or two.

'No, Rhys you cannot really believe that. It's not possible. Right, I'm sitting down now, are you sure this hasn't turned into one of the boozy sales conferences that "bloody man", your boss makes a habit of?'

'Love, I haven't had a drink, except the coffee. I am absolutely serious. Those comments are made by someone who is more than a sister, they are heart-breaking, writing down the things she wishes she could say to her daughter, but can never betray what was obviously a promise to her parents to let them bring Jane up as their own.'

'Ree. I'm sorry, I can't take all this in. You know I trust you absolutely and you wouldn't say any of this if you weren't sure in your own mind, but I need to process what all this would mean if it were true. And I do need that coffee.'

'For one thing it would mean Dot wasn't my aunt, she was my grandmother. I've already told my people I must leave on urgent business and the hotel are booking me out. I'll be home in a couple of hours, I know you'll need to see the evidence, but, yes, I am convinced it is true.'

'Ree, thanks for coming home, but please concentrate on the driving, try not to worry, if it's been true for fifty years it can wait another couple of hours. And stop and get a sticky bun. Oliver and I love you.'

39 Hopes Dashed

If the rush to the hospital for Oliver's birth was the most traumatic drive of his life, Rhys was sure this easily qualified as the second most traumatic. It wasn't only the revelation itself; it was how Anne would take it. Ever since they had found out that Dot had had a child, a daughter, it had been tearing at her heart through pregnancy, and now through motherhood.

Would she see what he now saw so clearly? Should he have waited, slept on it, read it again in the morning? And even if she agreed with him, it was only their instincts, maybe wanting it to be true. Was the single photo, with its inscription, proof enough?

He stopped at a service station, he needed the toilet after all that coffee, and bought his comfort food, forcing himself to sit, with unseeing eyes until the last speck of white icing was picked up by a wetted finger from the serviette. His tiredness had long since gone, but the sugar rush was welcome to make him concentrate on the dark roads, thankfully quieter after nine o'clock.

Seeing his headlights swing on to the drive, Anne was out of the house and in his arms as soon as the car door closed.

'Hey, look out, you'll squash the box.'

'Mr Silk.'

'What, you think you are having a hug with Mr Silk?' Rhys had every right to be confused.

'Whatever you and I think, and I haven't seen the notes yet, but let's suppose we agree, we need confirmation – proof. Mr Silk will have to open Dot's sealed box now, and that will contain the proof.'

'Hold on, let's get inside. You take this box while I dump my work stuff in the study. And I think a soothing cup of tea would suit us both. You've been crying, haven't you?'

'New mothers are apt to get emotional, it's hormonal. You and Gerry were always saying it was my hormones when it wasn't. Now it is, so watch out.' And she laughed as she cupped his face in her hands and drew him towards her for a long kiss.

'I hope you aren't intending to use that as an inducement to Mr Silk to open the box, I could see his wife chasing you up the street with her maracas and a bottle of sangria.'

'No, just for you, for being you and caring enough to drive home because you knew what it means to me to find Dot's child.

'Now, let me read these messages in peace, probably several times, and then I'll tell you what I think.'

Long before that the tears started again, and Rhys hugged her without saying a word.

Finally, Anne dried her eyes.

'I suppose you didn't bring one of those disgustingly sweet and fattening Belgian buns home with you?'

'I did, do you want half then, including the cherry?'

'Yes, please. I think you're right, Dot is talking to a daughter, not a sister. And those words on the back of the photo, they clinch it. I mean, they're sisters so they could look alike, but the words ... How on earth will you tell your mum?'

'First things first. Tomorrow I was due to be returning from the meeting, so I've gained half a day. In the morning I will phone Mr Silk and see if we can go to his office and look in the box. Only then do I think it is wise to tell Mum. When we have proof. But how did they do it? How did Dot's mother suddenly pop up with another child without any sign of being pregnant?'

Anne was thinking about Dot. 'How did she manage to keep her pregnancy a secret? OK, in the first few months it would be easy if you lived by yourself, but later? And where is the birth certificate? I trawled all the stuff on Ancestry.com that I could find. Even if the child had been registered under Dot's mother's name there should have been a certificate. And a doctor would have to have been in on it, for a price, I'll bet.'

They sat, side by side, each with half a bun and half a cherry, and another cup of tea.

'What about the house? I know Mr Silk said the Park is definitely left to you, but Dot's house was bought with her husband and should go to her only child, Jane, your mum.'

'I know, and you're right, Mum should have it, I doubt she would want to move, but the rents from the flats she might want to do something with. We might have to contribute to your dad's flat rent as we'd simply balanced it against his gardening skills and doing odd jobs.'

'Oh, God, I'd forgotten about that. And Mum is living there as well now. In a way it would be the best news ever to have found Dot's child, but it could become complicated.'

The complications started the next day.

Mr Silk was adamant. 'I'm sorry Mr Banks, your phone call has come as quite a shock, and I'm sure the evidence you have described will be as persuasive as you have said. But, your aunt's instructions, in writing, are that I can only consider an application to open the box if the person claiming to be her daughter is present. You will have to tell your mother and ask her if she wants to apply to open the box, and if so, she must demonstrate a compelling reason for me to do so.

'Having said that, the long association with both your aunt and yourself gives me confidence that, if the evidence is as you described, a favourable outcome is likely.'

'He said we have to get Mum there and he will probably open the box.' Rhys paraphrased for Anne when he came off the phone.

'Oh, hell. I thought we could get it all confirmed before we approached her, now we have to say we think it is true. How are you going to do this, Ree?'

'Compared to Dot, Mum might seem a quiet person, but she is very resilient and resourceful. She was a personal assistant to a couple of high-powered CEOs when she was working, and they were pretty demanding. What I'm sayings is, if we tell her straight and show her the evidence we have then, yes, she will be shocked, but she won't collapse and need smelling salts.'

'Smelling salts, what on earth are smelling salts?'

'I don't know, I've never seen them, but apparently they were wafted under the noses of young upper-class maidens who were inclined to faint at the mere mention of something distasteful, like an uncovered pianoforte leg.'

'You are having me on?'

'No, it's in all the best Victorian bodice-rippers.'

'My God, Ree there is obviously a side to your youth that we need to discuss. But not now. Do you think we ought to meet round at their house, Mum and Dad could look after Oliver for a couple of hours, I expect?'

40 Bad Reaction

Dealing with the whims and demands of business executives may have left Jane unflustered, telling her that her parents were not her parents, that her sister was not her sister but her mother, and that no one had the faintest idea who her real father was, that affected her very deeply. She wept for Dot, she wept for her "parents" and she wept for herself, and she said they should never have told her.

Rhys and Anne were distraught and got up to go, but she waved them down and calmed down with Bill's arm tightly round her and gripping his hand.

'Sorry, I didn't mean that. It's just so overwhelming. You were right to tell me, if I'd found out later that you knew I would have been very angry.

'That picture, it's the only one I know with both of us in it, somehow no one ever got us in the same place when there was a camera around. I can see why now. If you look carefully, I am looking at the camera, but Dot is looking at me. My God, what agonies those times must have been for her.'

'Mum,' Rhys spoke very quietly, 'I'm sorry, there was no easy way to tell you about this. Are you saying that you accept that Dot was your mother just from what we have shown you? There could be more evidence in the box at the solicitors, but we don't know. Even Mr Silk doesn't know what's in there, apart from a birth certificate.'

Before answering, Jane asked Bill to get some more tea for them all. She sat, seeing, and saying nothing, much as Rhys had done in that hotel bedroom.

When they all had a fresh cup of tea, she looked up and her face was serene under the tear stains.

'Dot was nineteen years older than me and had a very busy and successful working life during which she had a happy marriage. I didn't see much of her which was perfectly natural to me, but there were always birthday and Christmas presents, often generous amounts of money, which Mum made me save. I will keep calling them Mum and Dad because that's what they were to me.

'I met Bill, we married and had you. Dot never forgot your birthday and there were always presents at Christmas. Mum died and, shortly after so did Dad, I got the house in Birmingham and a chunk of money and shares, Dot got the Park and the same money and shares. We both sold the shares, and I sold the house and bought this one. I thought Dot would sell the Park, but it became her family after her husband died. Now I can understand why. The Park was the child she never really had. She couldn't bring me up but, by God she used to lecture the Park Mothers on how to bring up their children.

'I suppose, what I am saying is, Mum and Dad were always kind to me, a bit strict but they were already set in their ways when I came along, nineteen years after Dot. I can see how Dot being pregnant by a boy who didn't stick around would have been hugely embarrassing for them socially, and they would see it as ruining Dot's life as well.

'So, yes, I can see that Mum having the baby would appear to solve everything. Although how they did it, I have no idea.'

Anne had sat, staring at the floor since Jane's initial, shattering reaction. Now she looked up and wiped the moisture off her face with the back of her hand.

'That's the bit I cannot get my head round. I cannot find any birth records for you, yet you must have a birth certificate. That's the only thing Mr Silk was told was in the box.'

'I have, but did you know I was born in Scotland? Different registration district to England and Wales so if that is where you looked no wonder you couldn't find me.'

Rhys looked puzzled, 'Why were you born in Scotland when you lived in Birmingham?'

'I was told that Mum was up there for some time looking after an elderly relative, so that was where I was born. The relative died and Mum and I came back home.'

'So that's how they did the switch!' Rhys was impressed. 'Dot met her up there and they bribed some doctor to sign the details to fit the requirements.'

'Maybe. I'm sure you are right, with this photo and what is says on the back. But it is a terrible shock and I need to think it through because it turns my whole life upside down. So many conflicting thoughts, who am I when half of my parents are unknown? What did Mum and Dad give up to spend eighteen years raising me before I flew the nest to uni? What did Dot suffer watching me grow up without being able to be a mother?

'It's all going round and round in my head, I need time to discuss it with Bill, after all he married an unknowing fraud. I will speak to you tomorrow, in the meantime I'm sorry I snapped at you, you did the right thing by Dot and by me.'

Oliver received even more cuddles than usual when he was collected from Diane and Joseph. They were concerned at the obvious preoccupation of his parents, but Anne assured them there was nothing wrong, just a bit of a shock and she would phone the next day.

Anne couldn't sleep, she kept blaming herself for pursuing Dot's baby when Rhys had told her not to get so upset over it. And now she might have caused a rift in his family and probably opened a Pandoras box of unnecessary complications for everybody. Her mood infected Oliver and he was fractious, eventually waking Rhys.

At three o'clock they sat in the kitchen, Anne nursing the baby, Rhys with a mug of tea and working his way through a whole packet of chocolate biscuits.

'It's a mess, but it's not of your making. My grandparents' generation were still stuck in the Victorian era of public horror at babies born out of wedlock, and private acceptance of entitled men being able to do as they liked and then either pay off the unfortunate woman or simply sack them if they were a servant. I'm not saying my grandparents were like that, but they were brought up by parents who lived through that era of hypocrisy. In the 1950s it would have bought shame on a middle-class household to have an unmarried daughter with a child. All you did was to discover that situation, not create it.

'And Mum and Dad will deal with it, I dare say there were a lot more tears after we left, but at least we're not dealing with a stranger coming into the family.'

'If it's true. I know you're convinced Ree, and that photo is strong evidence, but what if we open the box and find it's somebody else? Perhaps it would be better not to ask Mr Silk to open the box.'

'I am one hundred per cent convinced, but it's not our decision anymore. Only Mum can ask for that box to be opened.

'Come on, Oliver has gone back to sleep, I've just eaten my way through heaven knows how many calories, and we both need our bed. It will look different in the morning.'

'Rhys? It's Mum, I've phoned Mr Silk and arranged to go to his office at ten o'clock Saturday morning. Obviously, I want you and Anne to be there. Could you arrange babysitting again, it might get a bit emotional for Oliver?

'And I'm sorry about the other night, I should have thanked you, not jumped down your throat. And tell Anne, whatever happens, I do appreciate how much she cared about Dot's baby.

'Call me when you get this message, unless you are driving, even with hands-free wait until you stop.'

41 All is Revealed

Mr Silk was at his most officious in keeping with the importance of the occasion, although his wife and secretary was obviously suppressing great excitement. The request by Jane Banks was formally noted and scissors were used to cut the sealed string holding the lid of the two feet cube box. Irrelevantly, Rhys noted with satisfaction that it was made by his firm.

The lid being lifted clear revealed another layer of cardboard with an envelope addressed to 'Mr Silk or his successor.' Frowning slightly, the solicitor opened the envelope and took out a single white card, he read it and smiled.

'The card says, If the person claiming to be my daughter is Jane Banks, neé Flower, then you can proceed with opening the box. If it is not Jane Banks, then the box must be resealed unopened. Signed Dorothy Jacks neé Flower.'

A huge sigh of relief filled the room, accompanied by a squeal from Mrs Silk and a 'How exciting.' Even her husband visibly relaxed, beamed at the family and lifted the cardboard to reveal a jumble of small toys, papers, school reports, and big envelopes.

Mr Silk walked around the desk and stood before Jane for a moment, 'I never thought I would see this day, but I am so happy that I could carry out what was the last of your mother's wishes. Mrs Silk and I will leave you now but when you want, we will have light refreshments and drinks in the new interview room next door.'

After much hugging and tears they all stood aside for Jane to go through the items in the box. It was an emotional journey through her youth, but the most poignant and tearful discovery were the envelopes full of Christmas and birthday cards, written but never sent. They didn't stop until Dot's death when Jane was fifty-six. Half a century of pent-up love and grief expressed for the first time to her daughter.

At the bottom of the box was another envelope in which Dot described how the arrangements were made for her mother to claim Jane's birth, the pressure put upon Dot, and the agreement she had to make to stop the baby being put up for adoption through one of the unregulated adoption societies if she didn't agree.

It was some time before they joined Mr and Mrs Silk, where tea had been supplemented by some alcoholic support. Rhys shook Mr Silk's hand and congratulated him on his handling of the delicate matter. Anne hugged the tearful Ethel Silk and kissed Mr Silk, much to his embarrassment, but only on the cheek.

Steering Mr Silk away from the crowd around the box, Rhys asked him to clarify the position of the house, should it be his mother's as the direct descendent of Dot?

Apparently, there was no question of this, the house was bequeathed as a direct result of Rhys fulfilling Dot's condition on keeping the Park running rather than selling it or going bankrupt in the specified time. It was, of course, entirely up to Rhys whether he wanted to share or transfer ownership to anyone, and Mr Silk would be pleased to draw up any agreement along those lines.

The group parted with more hugging and kissing and an agreement to all get together the next day, including Diane and Joseph, at Anne and Rhys's home.

It was there, for the first time, that Diane and Joseph,

rather self-consciously holding hands, learned of the fractured family history that had driven Dot to create the community in the Park that was to encompass not only her love of children, but also her acceptance of a man teetering on the edge of society.

And it was there that all the family learned how Anne and Rhys had turned down a fortune to make sure that Dot's vision could continue.

Follow the Dot's...

I do hope you enjoyed *Dot's Secret*, the third book in The Park trilogy. If you came upon this book without reading *Dot's Legacy,* and *Dot's Surprise* then look forward to catching up on two more years of Dot's history disrupting the lives of Rhys, Anne and everybody around them.

A very different book, *The Future Brokers,* written with my fellow writer, Dawn Knox, takes us into the future, but not too far. The year is 2050 and World leaders are not delivering on their climate change promises. A computer programmer, thrown out of work by Artificial Intelligence, is gravely injured falling down a mountain. His sight is restored, and he is fitted with a state-of-the-art prosthetic arm, then suddenly head hunted by a mysterious government department, with a very driven, and attractive boss. But who, or what, is the puppeteer that puts them in so much danger? Climate fiction wound round a love story enclosed in a thriller. Read the Reviews on Amazon, this is not Science Fiction with spaceships and aliens – and it could happen in your lifetime!

Do you enjoy travelling? By car, train, plane, motorhome, ship, bike, armchair? Then look on Amazon to find *Transport of Dreams* my short story book which takes you from Paris to Bangkok, from Seine Pirates to Sex and the Single Camper, individual stories to be dipped into as you travel as far as your imagination will take you.

All these books are available on Amazon as paperbacks and Kindle, search for Colin Payn, and find my books, all with five-star reviews.

Dot's Legacy: mybook.to/DotsLegacy

Dot's Surprise: mybook.to/DotsSurprise
Dot's Secret: mybook.to/DotsSecret
The Future Brokers: mybook.to/TheFutureBrokers
Transport of Dreams: mybook.to/TransportofDreams

Keep up to date with new projects at my website: colinpaynwriter.com and Facebook page: Colin Payn Writer. One final request, whatever you think of my books please tell others by writing a Review on Amazon, your comments are eagerly read as I work at finding ways to improve my writing craft.

Colin Payn

Printed in Great Britain
by Amazon